SURE SHOT

Also by Nicholas Osborn

Bullets Trilogy

A Day Late and a Bullet Short

Three Bullets to the Wind

Another Day, Another Bullet

Bullets Legend

The Coward Rob Ford

The Fighting Earps

SURE SHOT

Bullets Legend

Book 3

NICHOLAS OSBORN

Sure Shot
Paperback Edition

Wolfpack Publishing
1707 E. Diana Street
Tampa, Florida 33610

www.wolfpackpublishing.com

Paperback ISBN 979-8-89567-425-3
Ebook ISBN 979-8-89567-424-6
LCCN 2026938225

SURE SHOT

Chapter 1

You can't miss if you only have one bullet.

These were the words that played over and over and over again inside of Phoebe's mind. Told to her by her father, whose father told him, and so forth for five generations now. They were every bit as true today as they were when they were first uttered. A bullet was the difference between life and death, whether it hit its target or not. The only thing you could control was whose death was at hand.

She'd gone out to begin her hunt when the morning's light first broke. There was a chill in the air that followed her breath deep into her lungs, making her yearn for the sun's warmth on her skin. As her father's command echoed through every action, she moved deeper into the piney woods they called home, keeping her eyes trained on the branches above, her trigger finger extended out until she was ready to fire, just like she was taught. Her footsteps were silent, so was every exhale. She traced her way through the trees like she'd planted them herself, even though every one of them was easily twice her age.

In her hands was a Winchester 1873. Like most things in her life so far, it was given to her by her father. He didn't say much when he put it in her hands, but he expected the world, and he made that clear. It was just a rifle to most, a tool or a weapon, only as capable as the person pushing its stock against their shoulder. There were faded engravings on its wooden furniture, and the steel had blued with age, but its trigger was light, and its 44-40-caliber bullets could travel farther than most would believe. It was a lever-action capable of holding at least thirteen rounds comfortably. She had one. That single bullet would decide whether her family ate dinner or not.

In front of her was the same path that had been trodden a thousand times over in her twelve years of life. She'd come to know every leaf, every root, every hole, and every twist. She knew every branch that could hold a squirrel's weight, and she knew just where to place a shot to make sure it never had the chance to see for itself. Ahead of her was the path to something worth eating, and food meant security. It meant one more restful night's sleep, and even though she was just a child herself, she knew it meant one more chance to see another sunrise.

Behind her was the kind of person who didn't have to worry about any such things in life.

Even so, the boy was her best friend. She'd known him her whole life, what else could she call him? He hunted with her even when he didn't have to, and not only that, they'd done essentially everything together since they were old enough to take on chores. In that time, they'd developed the uncanny ability to talk to one another without saying a word.

Phoebe had listened to enough of his dragging feet. Every leaf that crunched and stick that snapped beneath his boots was another wasted opportunity. It was the perfect time to use such an ability, because if he couldn't walk quieter, her family wouldn't have anything to look forward to that evening.

She turned and said everything she needed to say with a simple glance. The boy, who carried the name Butler just like his own father, knew exactly what it meant. His knees lifted higher, and his boots came off the ground in an instant.

Phoebe was satisfied enough and went back to the hunt at hand. A breeze whispered through the trees, barely brushing against their cheeks. The sun started its routine climb over the horizon, allowing its light to give Phoebe a better chance to make her one bullet count. Birds chirped and fluttered in the distance, pine cones fell like rain into piles of leaves on the ground in every direction. To some, it was a quiet, serene moment in nature. To Phoebe, it was a roaring cacophony of life and death competing and coexisting, clashing in unison. It was up to her to single in on the most important detail before ever raising her Winchester.

Her eyes darted upward, scanning the canopy where the squirrels liked to bounce to and fro. Her grip on the rifle tightened, its weight a familiar anchor against her shoulder. She could feel Butler's presence behind her, quieter now, but still a half-step too loud for her liking. He was trying, she'd give him that at least.

A flicker of movement caught her eye. It was a

gray silhouette sprinting along a pine branch, its tail twitching like a taunt meant only for her. She raised the rifle, slow and deliberate, her finger still pointing forward, nowhere near the trigger just yet. The squirrel paused, oblivious to what most would call a child who stood below, holding its fate in her hands.

Her father's words rang clear, *you can't miss*.

She lined up the shot, her heart beat as steady as her breath. The world narrowed to the squirrel, the bead at the end of the rifle, and the moment at hand.

"Betcha I coulda already dropped that one," Butler whispered, his voice low but laced with the kind of smugness that wore a welcome thin.

Phoebe's jaw clenched, her focus broken. She didn't turn, didn't acknowledge him, but the squirrel spooked, skittering up the trunk and out of sight. Her chance was gone. She lowered the rifle, her chest tight with frustration, and shot Butler a glare that would keep him up at night.

"You tryin' to starve us?"

Butler grinned, unbothered, his eyes glinting with mischief. He was a year older than her, taller by a head, with a close-cropped haircut that reeked of expendable income. His own rifle—a shiny new Marlin, a gift from his family who never seemed to run out of money—hung loose in his hands, like it didn't matter if he ever fired off a shot.

"Relax, Phoebe. There's plenty more squirrels out here. Ain't like y'all are gonna go hungry just 'cause I was right about somethin'."

"You don't get it," she snapped, turning back to the path. "You never do."

Butler's family had a three-bedroom home, a pantry full of food, and a family that didn't have to claw and scrape for every meal. He hunted for sport, for bragging rights, while Phoebe hunted to keep her family alive. That difference sat between them like a barbed wire fence, and every so often, one of the two would prick themselves. It was a stark reminder that their lives were more different than they realized.

They moved deeper into the woods, the air getting thicker as the pines closed in around them. The sun was still creeping in the east, its light fighting to reach the ground through the branches overhead. Phoebe's steps were careful, she moved from heel to toe with silent ease, her eyes scanning for one more chance, one that she knew could be her last. Butler followed, his boots softer now, but she could still hear the faint rustle of his clothes, the occasional clink of his jacket buttons smashing against the rifle tucked too close to his belly. He'd become her best friend, for better or worse, but sometimes she wondered why she let him tag along. He always had to make it a competition, always had to talk when silence was what she needed most, always had to point out their glaringly obvious differences—like the fact that she had to grow up first.

"Phoebe!" Butler's whisper was urgent.

She followed his gaze to a low branch where another squirrel perched, carelessly lingering like there wasn't a rifle in sight to be trained on its meager existence out in the woods. It was a clean shot, maybe thirty yards out, but the light was tricky, filtering through the trees in patchy beams. She raised the old Winchester again, her movements fluid, rehearsed, just like she had been taught time and time again. Her finger itched to curl around the trigger as the rifle's worn stock found its familiar home snug against her cheek. She had to wait for the right moment.

Just when she was ready to move her finger to the trigger and flatten her finger in the final motion needed to come home with something to eat, the squirrel sensed something it didn't like. It turned to face Phoebe, and her heart sank. It leaped from one branch, darting back and forth, jumping erratically, and barely sticking every landing. It fought its way through the tangled branches, trying desperately to escape a fate it didn't know was trailing right behind its every step. The squirrel chirped and scrambled, getting further and further from sight, but Phoebe held steady.

Her rifle drifted lazily, panning to the right. Both of her eyes remained wide open, like she didn't even need to blink. The end of the rifle wasn't trained on the squirrel, or trying to follow where it had just been a second before, it was tracing a path where it was about to be. Phoebe allowed her instincts to take over, aiming not for her target, but where she knew her target would be. All she had to do was unleash flame and gunpowder and lead, and let the world do the rest.

She exhaled, slow and controlled, then squeezed the trigger. What was once just a barely audible scamper of a squirrel through the trees turned into a boom that left both her and Butler's ears ringing in the blink of an eye. The crack of the shot split the morning air, echoing through the trees and sending birds scattering in every direction. It was like a lightning strike in the quiet before a storm.

The bullet found its target midair, and the squirrel dropped like a dead weight in the ocean, tumbling from the branch above their heads to the leaves at their feet with a soft *thud*—sudden and final. It twitched for a few seconds, then lay still. Phoebe's lips slowly began to form a small, satisfied smile. One bullet, one kill, her dad would be beaming with pride, just like he always was when she returned from the woods with dinner dangling from her belt.

"Nice shot," Butler said, his tone grudging but genuine. He slung his Marlin over his shoulder and started toward the squirrel like he was the one who'd fired off the bullet that took its life.

Phoebe was already moving, though. She knelt beside the squirrel that had already taken its last breath, checking to make sure the shot was clean. Within a few seconds, she had grabbed it by the tail and tied a string around its tail, fastened to her belt. It hung lifeless at her side as she finally made eye contact with Butler. Its weight tugging at her hip was a small victory.

"Not bad," Butler teased, catching up to her. "Bet I'd have had two by now, though."

Phoebe rolled her eyes, wiping her hands on her jeans. "You'd have missed and scared off everything worth eatin' from here to Daingerfield if I woulda let you shoot."

"You're gonna regret sayin' that." Butler's grin widened as he raised his Marlin, scanning the trees with exaggerated swagger. "Watch and learn, Phoebe Anne." He always called her that when he wanted to rile her up, knowing it was the name her dad used when he was proud of her.

She didn't rise to the bait, just crossed her arms and watched as he took aim at nothing in particular, his posture all show and no substance, something that matches his ego uniquely well. It just wouldn't do.

"Remember, Butler. A bullet'll kill anything in its path. You gotta shoulder the stock tight, leave both eyes open, focus on the bead at the end of the barrel, and squeeze, don't pull the trigger. You have to shoot where the target is gonna be, not where it's at. That's the only way you'll put food on the—"

"Phoebe! Phoebe!"

They each paused at the words bouncing off the trees, interrupting Phoebe's impromptu shooting lesson. They cocked their heads to the side to make sure what they knew they heard was actually real.

"Get back here! Now!"

Phoebe was sprinting home before she even realized what was happening. She knew it was her mom's voice, but it was raw and hoarse, unlike anything she'd ever heard before. She could feel it deep in her gut—something was horribly wrong.

Her stomach dropped a little further with each frantic step. She managed to exchange a quick glance at Butler, who'd lost his cocky grin in an instant. He was a few steps behind her, doing his best to catch up as he crashed through yaupon and greenbrier. She wanted to know everything right then and there about what was happening, but she was still so far, the wait was killing her already. There was no time to slow her pace for Butler to catch up. The last time she looked behind her, Butler was sprawled out over the leaves on the ground, trying to pick himself up without limping. But Phoebe was running too fast now, she couldn't stop.

A clearing finally opened up ahead, and a few seconds later, their small cabin came into view. Phoebe's mom was standing on the porch, her face pale, her hands cupped around her mouth as she shouted hopelessly into the distance.

It didn't take long for Phoebe to notice that just beside her were two men in uniforms, badges glinting in the morning light and pistols tucked neatly at their sides. Phoebe's heart thudded as she slowed to a sudden stop, her grip tightening on the Winchester until her knuckles were bright white.

Butler skidded to a stop beside her, his breath ragged.

"Is that the cops?" he asked between pants.

"I think so."

"Don't you want to see what they're doin'?"

"I'm scared," she admitted. "Those red and blue lights flashin' without any sirens never mean anythin' good."

"It'll be all right," said Butler, putting his arm around her. "You ain't alone."

She afforded herself the slightest smile at her friend. They were young in heart and mind, but life was going to catch up to them in the worst of ways, whether they wanted it to or not. There were few kids who could have the foresight Phoebe had, and even fewer who could do what was necessary. Before the police could have a chance to break her heart, she went ahead and broke it herself.

"Take this," she said, pushing the rifle in her hands to Butler.

"No way. I ain't takin' your gun. Your dad'll kill me. I know how much it means to y'alls family."

"You think the cops are gonna let a twelve-year-old girl keep a rifle if somethin' happened to my dad?"

"You don't know what happened. Could be nothin'."

Phoebe shot the boy next to her a look that could've dropped him dead right where he stood. Instead, he thought better of his own words and reached out to take her rifle.

"I'll take yours, you can afford another one," she said, garnering a scoff from Butler. "Just for now, if it's nothin', we'll trade back later."

"I wish I was as smart as you sometimes."

"I wish I was as rich as you."

Their conversation trailed off into the breeze. One more hurried scream from her mom would send Phoebe running down the hill, weaving through trees, trying to reach the front porch of their cabin as fast as her legs would take her.

"Phoebe, honey," her mom said as soon as Phoebe was close enough to her voice. "It's your dad. He's gotta go away for just a little while, so he can talk to these nice policemen."

"What did he do?"

"He didn't do anythin'," her mom tried to reassure her.

"He's been arrested in connection with a cartel drug shipment that recently came through town," the fatter of the two officers said without an ounce of remorse.

"You can come see him tomorrow down at the jail," the other one spoke up, shooting a rude stare at his partner.

Phoebe's world tilted. "That's a damn lie!" she shouted, stepping forward. "My daddy don't do drugs! Mom, you gotta tell them!"

"Honey…" Her mom drifted off, unsure of what to say next, but still stifling the anger boiling in her belly at the cops who'd shown up unannounced. All she could do was let out a sob instead, though.

"They can't do that," she hollered. "It ain't right!"

"Who's the boy?" The fat officer lifted his finger to the edge of the wood line.

"That's just her little friend," Phoebe's mom let out. "He's from the Butler family, he didn't do anything."

"Leave him out of this!"

"Phoebe, please," her mom begged.

The cop's eyes slowly found their way to the rifle Phoebe was holding in her hands. It was an impressive Marlin, pristine and untouched, impossible to ignore. At the very least, it was nice enough to warrant their attention.

"What you got there?" one of them asked.

"Is that yours?" The other followed.

"Yes."

"What were you doing with that out there?"

As much as Phoebe wanted to raise it to her shoulder and bust her dad free from the grip of the law, she was raised better than that. She had to come clean.

"We were squirrel huntin', like we do every Wednesday mornin' durin' the season."

"Right."

"And you let them do this?" The fat officer gestured toward Phoebe's mom.

"Not everyone has as much to eat as you," Phoebe shot back before her mom could respond.

The officers got themselves a laugh out of Phoebe and her mom's misery. Their amusement was something that would be burned into the little girl's psyche until she grew old and died. The sound of their chuckles would keep her up at night. Phoebe could only watch their shoulders bounce up and down through the thick body armor beneath their uniform as they walked back to their patrol SUV parked in the driveway.

She couldn't make out the tears streaming down her dad's face, or the three letters he mouthed over and over again, or the fear that had taken hold in his eyes. All she could see was the silhouette of her dad. He lingered for a couple seconds before they hauled him away without another word. She watched the tail-lights disappear in the distance as her entire world fell apart.

"I'll figure this out, baby," her mom whispered through sporadic heaves. "I'll fix it."

Phoebe nodded, her throat too tight to speak. Her eyes burned with tears, but the rage in her belly had turned white hot. She was too small to fight back, too young to speak up. She was simply in over her head. And when she turned to find Butler in the distance, hoping to retrieve her rifle, she saw only lonesome trees towering up against the rising sun. Her best friend was gone, just like her dad.

As her mom sobbed and struggled to stand upright out in the front yard—much less offer comfort to the daughter whose world had just been turned upside down—Phoebe was forced to come to a conclusion she couldn't bear.

She was alone.

Chapter 2

"It's called the least hunted bird in Texas for a reason."

"Most people can't even spell chachalaca, and even fewer could tell you it's a bird in South Texas that you are only allowed to hunt in four counties in the state. There is nothing particularly special about this little bird, other than how little people actually know about it. For those watching at home, think the size of a gangly chicken, with the voice of a thousand screeching hens somehow coming from one single bird. It might not be a five-star restaurant quality type of meat, but what it's lacking in distinction, it more than makes up for in rarity. That's right, this little sucker might be hard to shoot, but it's even harder to find, especially when it's buried in thorn scrub."

Butler had the fortune of becoming a late twenty-something household name in the world of firearms, hunting, outdoors, and the meat-eating man crowd. His unbelievable online content centered around impossible shots on impossible targets catapulted him to every kind of fame imaginable after college. He'd spent the last few years traveling the world, hunting just about any wild game trophy he could, and recording every second of it for his millions of fans. He'd been offered just about every deal Hollywood could muster up, but Butler wasn't that kind of man.

Butler was a humble winner, a gracious do-gooder, and a reluctant icon, or at least that's what his management agency told him.

He'd found himself covered head to toe in camo that didn't match the terrain, shooting a new video with people who didn't know his best angles, and tracking down a stupid bird that every local laughed at the slightest mention of. He was told time and time again the chachalaca wasn't worth his time, but all that did was make him want it even more. It wasn't about the meager meal it might provide him, it was about the payoff of the content it would give him. Tomorrow might be another hunt, another improbable tale or unlikely shot, but today it would have to be the unfortunate fate of the chachalaca.

The South Texas sun was known to be a mean bastard, and this day was no different. It was beating down on Butler's neck like it had a personal grudge, like it was being paid to track him down and make his life hell. Sweat beaded at his brow, but he knew better than to wipe it off. Cinematic was the word that was told to him the last time he was caught trying to ease some of the hardships of the hunt on camera. If there was nothing difficult about the kill, there had to be some sense of danger involved to keep people tuned in. If that meant he had to scale a mountainside, traipse across a river, or hack his way through the woods without so much as a complaint, then that's just what it was.

The Winchester 1873 cradled in his hands was covered in a patina that promised stories he'd never fully know. Its engravings were worn to ghostly, barely visible outlines, but its trigger was smooth and welcoming. He'd had it since he was a kid. It was given to him on a promise that felt like a lifetime ago now. The memory of the first time his hands held its weight was something he'd never forget.

"Butler, you plannin' on doing any shooting today or is it just me?" called his cameraman from behind a tangle of mesquite.

The man charged with capturing the impossible on film was named Lamar Burton, and he was about as green as it gets. He was born and raised in the middle of Dallas and let that fact be known every chance he got. He was the kind of guy who was more at home with a drone than a deer stand, and he swore up and down that he had a knack for capturing the best shots in all their high-def glory. What Butler had seen so far was less than impressive, but given the special circumstances that dragged him out in the sweltering sun, he'd have to do.

The rest of the crew consisted of a sound guy who quite unironically introduced himself as Mike, and a director sent by the agency named Edward Graham, who kept checking his phone for a signal every two minutes. They were trailing slow behind, grumbling on and on about the heat and the thorns and the bugs and whatever else they laid their eyes on.

"Patience, Lamar," Butler drawled, flashing the grin that kept followers sticking around even after he'd run out of bullets. "You don't rush a shot like this. It's about feelin' the moment, not forcin' it. Ya know?"

He adjusted his stance, boots sinking into the

sandy soil, and scanned the scrub for any sign of the chachalaca. The bird's screech was unmistakable, a godawful racket that could be followed by even the most incompetent of city folk. It was also notoriously elusive, flitting through the dense brush more like a memory than a chicken with a fancy name. Finding it was most of the battle, because once Butler could lay eyes on it, making the shot was as sure as sure gets.

Butler's process was simple, or at least that's what he liked to tell his fans. *Firm grip, focus on the bead at the end of the barrel, then squeeze the trigger. The trick is to shoot where it's going to be, not where it's at.* If there was such a thing as a catchphrase for Butler's on-screen personality, it was that process. He repeated it every show, like a mantra he couldn't escape from. It grounded him, made him believable, even when what he was doing was anything but.

He knew where it came from, deep down, but people didn't care about that. People cared about what he could do with it. Because of that, he'd built his whole career on those words, and a rifle that was never his to begin with.

Every impossible shot he'd ever made, from bagging an elk at a thousand yards to tagging a clay pigeon at a hundred yards—blind—Butler owed it all to a little girl he knew a lifetime ago. He would never admit such a thing on camera, though. His brand was built on being the guy who could do anything, not the guy who owed it all to a girl he hadn't seen in years.

A rustle in the brush snapped him out of his introspection. There it was, scrawny and awkward, perched on a gnarled branch more than fifty yards away. The stupid chicken. Its beady, black eyes were voids in the sunlight, its whole body flicked like it knew it was being watched. Butler's pulse slowed, his hands steadied.

"All right, folks," Butler said, his voice almost a whisper, picked up with crisp clarity by the tiny microphone clipped on the collar of his pearl snap denim shirt. "You might think that I dragged y'all all the way to the ass end of Texas for a bird called a chachalaca, and to some degree, that's exactly right."

He raised the Winchester, the stock settling in against his shoulder like an old friend. The worn wood felt like home on his cheek, the scent of gunpowder residue filled his nostrils.

"But that ain't the only reason," he said as he leaned his head down to rest on the stock.

His finger was straightforward, his eyes open, his target almost lined up on the bead at the end of the barrel. The shot was easy, and it was his for the taking, but that wasn't his claim to fame.

"This right here is what a rational hunter would be doin'," he continued. "He'd steady his breath, shoulder the stock tight, lean in with both eyes open, focusing on the sight at the end of the barrel and lining it up just right with your target, then squeeze the trigger, don't pull. Remember…" His voice trailed off just long enough to turn his gaze to the camera in Lamar's hands.

"Shoot where it's gonna be, not where it's at."

When he should have pulled the trigger and watched the bullet claim the life of that lone bird in the distance, he did what no one was expecting. He dropped the end of the rifle to the ground and released the stock from his shoulder.

"I never said I was rational, though," he smarted off.

He could feel Lamar, Mike, and Edward collectively roll their eyes and exhale a groan at his dramaticism. They may have been annoyed at his ego, but he knew this was what the fans were showing up for. He had to do the unexpected. He slung the rifle over his shoulder, put the chachalaca at his back, and faced the camera head-on.

"Y'all listen up," Butler said, his grin widening as he planted his boots in the sandy soil, the thorn scrub framing him like a stage. "You know I'm all about the impossible. Shots that make your jaw drop, hunts that make your heart race, and enough good looks to keep you comin' back for more. But what I got for you today ain't just about this scrawny bird behind me."

The chachalaca screeched again, right on cue, almost like he planned it from the start. Lamar panned over to the bird, then back to Butler, zoomed in, making sure to catch the glint in his eyes, the sweat on his brow, the confidence in his stance.

"Before comin' down south, I spoke to a man named Frank Rourke, who you might know better as the governor of the great state of Texas," Butler continued, his voice rising with the cadence of a preacher standing before a congregation. "He let me know they had somethin' up their sleeve to celebrate his recent election in November. Everyone told him he couldn't do it, that he was wastin' his time runnin' for office. We all saw how that worked out. He called me from Austin to tell me about an event this world hasn't seen since the days of Buffalo Bill Cody and his traveling Congress. It'll be the biggest shindig the state has ever seen, with rodeoin', barbecuin' off a chuck wagon, Grand Ole Opry-style performances, and more, all in honor of the state's bright new future ahead. And to top it all off, he's puttin' together the best hunters and enthusiasts in Texas to show off their skills in a shooting competition."

"What the—" Lamar turned to Edward and mouthed.

He was cut off by the universal sign to shut his mouth by the director, who was the only one who could sense Butler's intentions. This wasn't just another hunt for his channel, it was an announcement of something much larger.

"It's called the *Texas Sure Shot,* and let me tell y'all what, it's gonna be a spectacle to behold. We're talkin' trick shots that'll make your head spin, long-range targets that'll separate the men from the boys, and the kind of crowd that'll make Hollywood itself beg the governor to attend."

He paused, letting his gaze wander across the horizon as the sun did its best to blind him from actually seeing anything. He knew this was the kind of content that millions would be watching later, and he wanted his words to sink in. When he felt like enough time had appropriately passed by, and to the urging of his cameraman Lamar, he finally spoke up.

"And the spoils set for the victor of the first-ever *Texas Sure Shot* celebration and competition? It's a doozy. The winner gets one executive order request from the incoming governor himself. Whatever you want, within reason, of course. You wanna save a piece of land? Make your hometown the official barbecue capital of Texas? Sorry, Lockhart"—he gave a quick wink to the camera before picking up right back where he left off—"that's the kind of power we're talkin' about. If you've been under a rock for the last fifty years and don't know what an executive order is, just know that it's worth your time to brush up on those fundamentals and shoot your shot to become the first-ever winner of the *Texas Sure Shot.* Anyone can throw their hat in the ring, but only a few are gonna have what it takes."

Butler leaned even closer to the camera. "And here's the real kicker. The governor invited *me* to headline this whole thing. Me, Butler, the guy who can shoot anythin' that moves with my eyes closed. I tried to tell him it just wouldn't be a fair match if I was playin'," Butler found time for yet another wink. "He wasn't havin' any of that, though. So, I'm damn excited to be the first to break the news, I'll be headed to Austin with this ol' Winchester in hand this summer, to take on the best shooters Texas has to offer."

He patted the worn rifle still slung over his shoulder, its worn stock glinting in the sunlight. He couldn't help but notice that his crew had finally caught on to the real reason they were sweating out in the middle of nowhere. Lamar was practically vibrating with excitement, his camera steady despite the thorns snagging his jeans and jabbing his skin. Mike adjusted his boom nervously, catching every word with desperate intent, and Edward finally put his phone down, his eyes wide with dollar signs. Butler could feel the energy shift. This was a game-changer, a moment that'd rocket his brand to the stratosphere. All he had to do was pull off the impossible yet again.

"I've already got my personal request to the governor in mind, so if you wanna win it for yourself, you're gonna have to bring your best, and go through me."

After the final word slipped through his lips, he finally curled his finger around the trigger, brushing it gently, and without so much as the slightest flinch, he squeezed.

BAM.

The gunshot bounced through the woods and echoed all around them, the thorn scrub now more than just a home to a little bird, but a monument to behold what shouldn't be possible in this world. The rifle recoiled down into Butler's hands, he could feel the jarring blast of the bullet from the rifle supported only by the topside of his shoulder. He kept his eyes fixated on the camera in Lamar's trembling hands through it all, allowing the rifle's barrel to spew flame and smoke without even blinking.

One moment, the chachalaca was dancing through the thorns, minding its own business, content in its own obscurity. The next lead struck through flesh and bone, leaving only a puff of feathers floating in the air, and a dead bird lying in the dirt.

Chapter 3

It takes a certain kind of person to be up before the sunrise, trudging through the darkness, waiting on a promised light to guide the way, beginning their day before the earth could do the same.

The sun was half an hour from clawing its way over the horizon, but Phoebe was already crouched in the dew-soaked grass, her breath fogging in the predawn chill, her eyes twitching back and forth, desperate to find anything moving. The years had left her unchanged. It was still too early to be awake. She was still having to hunt for almost every meal. Her family was still a victim of a downright rotten lie.

She was older now, for whatever that was worth. She was more competent with a firearm than most people would ever believe was necessary. This had allowed her to do more than survive, too. Her mom had never left, and considering she didn't make enough money waitressing to keep the lights on, a meal that wasn't microwaved or stolen from work was hard to come by.

It was the reason she was out in the woods before the sun could rise over the eastern horizon. Whether her mom would ever admit it or not, the meat she could stock their freezer with was more often all they had to eat. It was fine as far as Phoebe was concerned, because she'd never admit to the sad truth that these moments were the best part of her day. Being alone in the trees, with the only thing driving every thought and action being how loud her belly was growling. It was simple, like how things ought to be.

There was nothing else simple about the life she'd been dealt. Her world was small, fenced in by necessity and unbearably desolate. She was still getting used to her twenties, and she still carried her father's words like a brand seared into her soul. *You can't miss if you only have one bullet.* Today, like most days, that one lonesome bullet was all she had.

Her hands gripped a beat-up Remington 514, a .22-bolt action with beat-up wooden furniture and an almost rusted bolt. The rifle was a far cry from the Winchester she'd lost so many years ago, but it had done its job well enough to put enough small game on their table to make it through several winters. The rifle was a thrift-store find, its barrel pitted, and its stock scratched to hell, but it was hers, and it shot straight enough, all things considered. She'd learned to make do, same as she'd learned to live with the ache in her chest where her father's words of wisdom used to live.

The Remington rested against her shoulder, its weight betraying the .22-caliber bullet already chambered inside the barrel. She zigzagged her way through the homestead that had become more of a patchwork of survival than a home worth raising a family on. A sagging cabin, a garden her mother tended just enough to yield a couple of tomatoes a year, and a stretch of woods that acted as more of a passage for squirrels to move through on their way to greener pastures.

Phoebe's eyes scanned the tree line. The first rays of light were just beginning to pierce through the tangled branches, glinting off leaves still wet from last night's rain. Her stomach growled again, a low rumble that forced her focus to remain steady. Her mother had spent the last of their cash on something she wouldn't speak about. Those were the types of things she chose to ignore to protect her own sanity. There were only so many problems she could solve with her own two hands.

A flicker of movement caught her eye, just the kind of distraction she was desperately hoping for. It was a whitetail doe, grazing at the edge of a clearing, maybe sixty yards out. Too far for most, but not for Phoebe. She'd been hunting since she was old enough to hold a rifle, and she'd learned to read the woods like a book written just for her. The doe's ears twitched, sensing something, but Phoebe was downwind, her body still as the cedars around her. She raised the rifle, slow and deliberate, her finger straight alongside the trigger guard.

In the state of Texas, she would be up shit creek if she were found hunting a deer with a rimfire bullet. It was illegal. Most people would say it was unethical, due to the fact that a humane kill is unlikely. They say it wouldn't do the trick, that it would cause unnecessary suffering and make tracking the game after being shot almost impossible.

Most people couldn't shoot like Phoebe, though. Most people also weren't so dependent on whatever happened to walk through their backyard to eat dinner, either.

She traced the doe through the trees for the next few minutes, letting it wander aimlessly, nibbling at nothing as it meandered around. She allowed herself to consider why such a shot is deemed impossible with a rimfire bullet like a 22. Hunters are told to hit just behind the shoulder, penetrating the vital organs and humanely dispatching the deer. A .22 bullet lacks the power to do such damage. This would require her to send the tiny bullet either through the deer's brain or through its brain stem. Only a perfect shot would make it happen.

It was times like this when she missed her old Winchester the most. It was like the rifle couldn't miss a shot, or at least that's how she fondly remembered it. The Remington was a fine gun, all things considered, but she had to try a lot harder. Luckily, she could still depend on her dad's words.

The doe tensed, almost ready to bolt away, and stared right at Phoebe. All of a sudden, time itself slowed to a crawl, and tunnel vision set in around her. They were locked in place together, sharing a moment that would soon turn sour with the squeeze of a trigger. The light was low, the distance tricky, and the Remington's sights were about as precise as a drunk's aim at a dartboard. Phoebe didn't have the luxury of doubt.

She exhaled, her breath steady, and let her instincts take over like they always did. She wished for the ancient hum of her old Winchester even while she rested her cheek against the beat-up stock of her .22 rifle. Pushing the thoughts of her dad that came with such wishes aside, she allowed her finger to curl onto the trigger at last. Her index finger flattened against the trigger, and she let all of the air out of her lungs. There wouldn't be another breath taken between her and her target before a bullet blasted out. Just when she thought she couldn't take another second without sucking oxygen, Phoebe squeezed the trigger as gentle as a whisper.

The crack of the shot split the morning, sending every bird in a fifty-foot radius exploding from the trees. Its echo lasted longer than the doe. It took only half a step before it collapsed into the leaves without so much as a shudder. It was a clean hit, right through the central nervous system collected at the top of its neck. The kill zone in such a spot was smaller than most people could see, much less shoot, but Phoebe's bullet tore through the spinal column with ease. The result was an instantaneous kill, quick and humane, even if the state of Texas would say otherwise.

Phoebe's lips curled into a small, hard-won smile. One bullet, one kill. Her father would've been proud, even if she had to explain why she wasn't using the rifle that was handed down to her so long ago. She slung the Remington over her shoulder and made her way to the doe lying still in the dirt, her boots sinking into the soft earth and crushing leaves and sticks and whatever might lie beneath them. The air smelled of damp pine mixed with the faintest trace of gunpowder still lingering in the barrel of her rifle, a scent that grounded her even as her thoughts drifted to the man who'd taught her to shoot. Her father, being dragged away in handcuffs, forced to rot in a cell for a crime she refused to believe ever existed. The memory of that day, the cops' smirks, her mother's sobs, her own sinking depression, burned in her chest like it just happened minutes ago, rather than years.

She kneeled down gently, her knife already in hand. The blade looked to be as dull as a butter knife, but it still cut clean, and she worked quickly, field-dressing the animal with the efficiency of someone who'd done it a hundred times. Blood stained her hands, warm and slick, but she didn't flinch. This was life, and if there was one thing she'd learned through the years, more often than not, it came at the hands of death. Survival wasn't pretty, but it was honest.

She wrapped the quartered venison in a cord she'd brought, tying it tight enough to hoist it over her shoulder. The weight was heavy, but it was a good kind of heavy, the kind that made her remember what a full stomach felt like. A grumble roared again as she started to walk back to their cabin. At least she could admire the dawn breaking over the horizon and its cotton candy streaks of orange and pink painting the sky. It wasn't long before their cabin came into view, its sagging roof and peeling paint looking even sorrier in the light of day.

Her mother was already up, kneeling in the garden, her hands buried in the dirt that refused to give them enough to eat consistently. She didn't look up as Phoebe approached, but the tension in her shoulders said she'd heard the shot.

"Got a doe," Phoebe called, setting the split pieces of deer she'd just broken down beside the porch. "Enough to eat on for a while, at least until the next check hits the bank."

Her mother nodded, wiping sweat from her brow with the back of her hand. "Good. Save the bones for broth." Her voice was flat, like she was reading from a script she'd memorized years ago.

Phoebe didn't push her. There were days when her mother spoke in full sentences, and days when she barely spoke at all. Today felt like the latter.

Phoebe hauled the meat inside, the cabin's single room smelling of mildew and the faint bitterness of yesterday's coffee still sloshing around in a pot beside the fireplace. The Remington went on its rack above the door, its barrel catching a glint of sunlight through the cracked window.

She washed her bloodied hands in the sink and, for a brief moment, reflected on the possibility that her own inability to save her father from his fate in a jail cell meant there was blood on her hands that was not from the deer. She shook the harrowing thought away and reached for the radio, an old battery-powered thing that crackled to life with a burst of static. It was their only connection to the outside world, and even that was spotty, picking up more static than signal most days. She fiddled with the dial, trying to find something other than gospel or country, when a voice cut through the noise, sharp and official, with the kind of Texas drawl that could have been pulled right out of an old-time radio program of *The Lone Ranger*.

"…and in a bold move to revive the spirit of the Wild West following his recent election, the Governor of Texas has announced an all-new one-of-a-kind shooting competition, with the kind of grand prize that most folks couldn't even imagine. An executive order, granted by the governor himself to whoever may claim that coveted top spot, within reason, of course. A chance to right a wrong, to change a life, to make history…"

Phoebe froze, her hand hovering over the dial. The radio voice went on, describing a spectacle unlike anything Texas had seen in a century. Trick shots, endurance rounds, long-range feats of firearms finesse, all backed by a festival of chuckwagons and rodeos, culminating in a single winner who could ask for anything the governor's pen could grant.

Her heart thudded in her chest. Freedom for her father. The thought hit her like a bullet, sharp and precise, burrowing into her mind. She could see him, his calloused hands teaching her to aim, his voice steady as he told her to trust her instincts. Deep down, the only thing her instincts were truly telling her was something she'd considered for far too long—he'd been framed. If she was right, that meant the men who'd put him there were untouchable, their influence stretching from the county courthouse all the way up to that pretty, pristine state capitol. But an executive order? That was power she could wield.

"So, come on down to Austin if you think you have what it takes to win the first-ever *Texas Sure Shot* competition and celebration. Registration is open for just five more days for anyone who can qualify. But a warning to the wise, the event's host and fellow competitor has been announced, and he will be stiff competition for sure. The one and only…"

The radio crackled again, the announcer's voice fading into static. Phoebe turned it off, the silence in the cabin heavier than before. She'd heard enough. If this competition was real, and the governor was truly granting a blank check to the winner, she could get her family back. Her mind raced at the possibilities, and she couldn't hold in her excitement. For the first time in what felt like years, Phoebe couldn't wait to talk to her mom and let her know what she'd just heard.

She stepped outside, where her mother was still in the garden, pulling weeds with a ferocity that suggested she was fighting something bigger than dandelions. Phoebe knew she had her own demons, just like everyone else, but she knew her mom's struggle stemmed from the same place as her own. Injustice had a way of taking hold when nothing else could.

"Mom," Phoebe said, her voice low but brimming with a newfound eagerness that she barely recognized. "I just heard something on the radio, and it felt like they were talkin' right to me. The governor's holding a shooting competition, and he's giving a request for an executive order signed by him as the grand prize. Anything you want. Can you believe that?"

Her mother didn't look up. "Don't start, Phoebe. Not today."

"I'm telling ya, I could win that whole dang thing. It might be our only way of ever getting Dad outta there."

This time, her mother's hands stilled, dirt caked under her nails. She sat back on her heels, her eyes narrow and sharp, like she was sighting down a barrel herself. "You think you can just walk into Austin and shoot your way to a miracle? You think they'll let you, a nobody with a thrift-store gun? Just give it up, Phoebe. Your dad is gone, and he ain't comin' back."

"I'm not a nobody," Phoebe snapped, the words out before she could stop them.

Her mother's face softened, but only for a moment. "That rifle you lost, Phoebe, it was different. You know it was. That one you're holdin' now ain't the same.

And you goin' out there, stirring up trouble, it'll only make things worse. For you, for me, for him."

Phoebe's jaw tightened. Her mother didn't choose to speak about anything relating to her father very often, and even less about that old rifle he gave her, but there was something in her tone now, a warning that went beyond caution. It was as if she knew something she wasn't ready to talk about, something she'd never shared before. When the silence became more than she could bear, Phoebe decided to speak up.

"You know I don't need that rifle," Phoebe said, though the words felt like a lie from the second they moved past her lips. "I've made do with less before. We both have."

Her mother stood, brushing dirt from her hands. "You go to Austin, you're not just risking yourself. Do you honestly think the men who put your dad behind bars for the rest of his life aren't out there still? If he really was caught up in all—"

"He wasn't!"

"Phoebe," her mom tried to reason.

"No. Stop it."

"You stop it, Phoebe. How many times do we have to go through this? If they see you—"

"Then let them see me," Phoebe cut her mom off once again, her voice steady as her aim. "I'm done hiding. I'm done scraping by. Dad's been in that cell for ten years. Ten years. If there's finally a chance to get him out, I'm taking it. I'm tired of livin' like this."

Her mom's eyes searched hers, and for a moment, Phoebe thought she saw a flicker of pride buried deep under the overwhelming fear welling up inside her. But then her mother turned back to the garden, her silence louder than any argument. Phoebe didn't wait for more. She walked back into the cabin, her boots thudding against the warped floorboards. The radio sat silent, but its message echoed in her mind. All she had to do was make it to Austin.

She glanced at the Remington, its scratches catching the light, and felt a pang of doubt. Was her mom right? Could she do it with this rifle, this battered relic that demanded every ounce of her skill? It was like the weight of her dad's old rifle was still in her hands as the thoughts raced through her mind.

Then, a fleeting face flashed across her eyes. A man she hadn't thought of in years, a decision she had made in the heat of the moment, one that she regretted for far too long. It took longer than she would ever admit to remember his name, but when it hit her, she lost the breath in her lungs and her knees trembled—Butler. The name twisted in her gut, a mix of righteous anger and hatred boiled inside her, before something softer began to rise up, something she didn't want to name. She swallowed all of her feelings as quickly as they had come up.

She didn't need the Winchester. She didn't need that man. Phoebe had everything she needed to win that competition, and it started with the words of her dad. There was a hunger inside her that went deeper than any empty stomach. She'd go to Austin, take her shot, then she'd bring her father home. Simple as that.

Phoebe grabbed a worn duffel bag from under the cot and started packing without hesitating a second longer. All she had was one change of clothes and the last of her cash tucked into an old metal coffee can that had been turned into a feed scoop for livestock they no longer owned. As she zipped the bag, her mother appeared in the doorway, her silhouette framed by the morning light creeping higher into the sky.

"You're really gonna go, aren't you?"

Phoebe didn't look up. "I have to."

"Then I guess you better win," her mother said, and there was steel in her words, the kind Phoebe hadn't heard in years.

Phoebe nodded, trying to avoid eye contact as she slung the bag over her shoulder. "Thank you, Mom. I promise I'm not gonna come home empty-handed."

"I know you won't," her mom admitted. "But take this just in case."

Her mom reached her fist out and uncurled her fingers to reveal a single bullet, its brass worn and aged. It was a bullet to a rifle she didn't own anymore, a .44-40 caliber that she knew all too well.

"Maybe there's a little bit of magic left in this old thing," her mom said.

Phoebe reached her hand out. As soon as the bullet was in her grasp, she grabbed her mom and squeezed her tight, never wanting to let go, but knowing it was the only way.

Chapter 4

Once again in her life, Phoebe was staring down the same woods that taught her how to carry the weight of a life that wasn't fair.

It was the same woods where she'd learned to shoot, to survive, to listen to the advice she'd carry throughout her entire life. These were the kind of woods that harbored everything, that refused to let go of who you were. They might not be the same trees, the same leaves, or the same dirt trodden beneath her feet. But they knew who Phoebe was, and they did not care about who she dared to become. They towered over her, no different than the policemen who came without warning, no different than the lies they told.

This time, there was hope, though. Somewhere in Austin, a chance to rewrite her story, and her family's story, was waiting for her to just take it. She took a deep breath and put one foot in front of the other.

The sun beckoned her forward with golden rays breaking through the branches overhead. What were once long shadows twisting and curling like demons on the dirt had been replaced with glorious beams of light guiding her every step. She'd have to trace her way through the woods that she'd survived off of for so long just one more time to find the highway that snaked through the state on the other side. Although hitching a ride was something she didn't have any experience with, she figured it was only the first of many risks she'd be forced to take on in order to arrive at the competition, much less win the whole thing.

Phoebe moved through the woods, her boots crunching on pine needles, her duffel bag slung over one shoulder, stuffed with the scraps of her meager life. A worn flannel, a pocketknife, a handful of crumpled dollar bills mixed with a couple dozen .22 rounds. The bullet her mother had given her that morning sat in her pocket, just so she could feel the weight as a reminder of what she was doing. The beat-up Remington 514 bolt-action hung in her hands chambered with only a single bullet, just like always.

Her heart pounded with the radio's promise of the governor's competition, a shot at freeing her father from a cell. For every dream she could conjure about its whispered opportunity, there were two nightmare realizations that it could all be for nothing. The only thing she could do was force all of the thoughts out of her head and focus on the task at hand. This time, it wasn't hunting for dinner or counting change on the kitchen table to see if they had enough to make it to the end of the week. This time, it was finding a way to the capital of Texas itself. Austin was calling.

She'd been walking for half an hour, zigzagging through the woods to reach a highway she'd only ridden a few times in her life. The humidity was heavy with the scent of damp pine and earth, and her ears were filled with the kind of quiet that made every snap of a twig sound like a gunshot. She was alone, the way she liked it, and she could find solace in the moment before her life was filled with unfamiliar views and uncertain decisions.

A boot pressing down on a leaf that wasn't her own broke the silence and her peace of mind, all at once. Phoebe froze. Not far ahead, another stick cracked in half, followed by a muffled curse and the rustle of leaves. Her heart sank to her stomach. Someone was out there, and they weren't trying to hide. The last thing she wanted to do was explain herself to a random passerby or have a dreadful passing conversation about the weather. She braced herself to muster up a halfhearted smile and pressed on.

It wouldn't be until she heard an all-too-familiar sound of a hammer clicking back on a revolver that she realized small talk was the least of her worries. Trouble had already found her, before she had gotten more than an hour's walk away from her home.

Phoebe dropped to a crouch, her eyes scanning the tree line. Frustration began to rise up from her gut when she was unable to find anything resembling a silhouette of a person, much less one pointing a gun at her. She gripped the Remington a little tighter, its battered stock pressed against her shoulder.

A voice cut through the pines before she could find anyone. His voice was more of a grumble, and it was greased with bad intentions. "Phoebe, right? No need for that rifle, girl. I'm only here to talk."

She pivoted, the Remington raised, her eye sighting down the barrel. A man stepped into the clearing, maybe thirty yards out, his revolver held low but cocked, his other hand raised in a mock gesture of peace. He was lean, with a weathered face and a cowboy hat tilted way back to reveal his oversized forehead. His eyes glinted with the kind of confidence that came from thinking he held all the cards. His jacket was dark, patched with dirt, and a knife hung at his belt. He didn't exactly look like a man who only wanted to talk.

"Who the *hell* are you?" Phoebe said calmly, even though her heart was pounding like a drum. "And how do you know my name?"

The man smirked, his revolver glinting against a flicker of light. "We know things. We know you're plannin' to head to Austin for that shootin' contest. My boss sent me to make you an offer." He took a step closer, his boots crunching on the forest floor. "Ten thousand bucks, cash, to stay home. No trouble, no fuss. You walk away, and you're richer for it."

Phoebe's jaw tightened. Ten thousand dollars was more than she'd seen in a year. It was enough to keep the lights on, to fill the fridge for a few months, but the offer would do nothing to accomplish what she was really after. The man did not make his offer out of gentle kindness. It was a bribe. He was here to stop her, and she'd be damned if she let him.

"I'm going to Austin," she said. "Keep your money."

The man's smirk faded, his eyes narrowing. "Wrong answer, girl. You don't know my boss, and that's fine, but what you do need to know is he sure as hell don't like bein' told no." He raised his revolver, not aiming yet, but the threat was clear. "Last chance. Take the money, or you'll never leave these woods again."

Phoebe's blood ran hot through her veins, her mind forcing her into fight or flight, even though she'd already made her decision on what would happen next. She just needed to wait for the man to quit talking. She'd faced down worse in her life. Hunger, loneliness, the memory of her father's arrest would take their toll on her long before this man had a say in what she would be doing. This man fancied himself a predator, sent by someone who knew impossible things. She thought of the bullet loose in her pocket and wished to feel the gentle hum of the Winchester at her shoulder again. She missed its promise to hit home against all odds. All she had was the old bolt-action .22 to carry her through, though. It would have to be enough.

"Walk away," she warned at last. "While you still can."

The man laughed, a harsh rasp that echoed through the pines. "You think that peashooter's gonna scare me?"

Time slowed as tunnel vision began to sink in. The distance was tricky. Thirty yards, with branches and shadows obscuring the shot, and a target as small as a fingernail wasn't anything to laugh at. The .22 she held in her hands wasn't made for stopping a man dead in his tracks. Most would call it impossible, and on any other day, Phoebe would've agreed with them, but that wasn't an option today.

She raised the Remington just as the man across from her began to lift his revolver in her direction. Her cheek hit the battered stock, and her eye traced down the length of the barrel in a fraction of a second. The man's revolver was steady, his finger curling toward the trigger as she moved. There was only one chance, and no room for doubt, just like she was used to. Her father's words rang in her ears one more time. She exhaled, then squeezed the trigger gently.

The shot cracked through the air like a whip that sent birds exploding from the trees. The bullet, small and deadly, sliced through the Texas heat, threading between yaupons to strike bone and flesh wrapped around the revolver's trigger.

In the blink of an eye, blood spewed into the air, painting the side of the revolver bright red, just as a faint *thump* hit the leaves. It took a second for the stranger to realize what had happened to him. For a moment, Phoebe could see the man still trying to fire a bullet of his own, before the grim realization set in. His trigger finger wasn't there anymore. He staggered back, his eyes wide with shock as he traced his own horror down to the appendage in the dirt that had been attached to his right hand only seconds before.

Phoebe worked the bolt back without hesitating, reached into her back pocket, and tossed another round into the open barrel, chambering it with a motion as natural as breathing.

"Drop it," she told the man before he had a chance to scream.

His revolver hit the dirt by the time the last word left Phoebe's lips. His hands were raised high into the air a second later, displaying all nine fingers as blood ran down his right arm. His bravado was long gone, replaced by the shocking realization that he'd gotten into something he couldn't finish. His jaw was slack, his eyes uncertain if they should focus on the garish wound on his right hand or the woman who'd just blown his finger off with a .22. All that could escape his mouth was an insult that wasn't worth his breath.

"You stupid fu—"

Phoebe gently leaned her head back on the stock of the rifle pushed to her shoulder.

"You blew my finger off!"

Her finger began to curl once more around the trigger as she ignored the man's desperate pleas.

"Okay, okay, okay." He tried to come to his senses while he could still think right. Panic had overtaken him, and the surge of adrenaline coursing through his veins made him tremble violently. "Don't you dare think this ends now," he sputtered. "Mr. Hearst will be waitin' on you, and he won't take kindly to this."

"You tell him I'm comin'," Phoebe said, her aim unwavering. "And if I see *you* again, I won't aim for your gun. You hear me?"

She wouldn't know whether he heard her or not, because in the blink of an eye, the man had turned and sprinted away. All she could hear was the pounding of his boots in the dirt and his hoarse panting. The faint trace of his curses faded into the pines as he disappeared into the distance.

Phoebe lowered the Remington at last and walked over to where the man had been standing. In his hurry to escape with his life, he'd left two things behind—a revolver covered in blood and a finger, still half curled, trying to find the trigger it never got to squeeze. It wasn't much, but what just happened was clear. Someone didn't want her in that competition. She knew sooner or later she'd find out who this Mr. Hearst was, but now she had to worry about what lurked behind every corner. Her heart sank at the thought of how much danger she'd be in, and it called to mind the apprehension her mom voiced so strongly.

The man's tracks were fresh in the dirt, a trail of broken twigs and scuffed leaves leading deeper into the woods. It was clear enough for a blind man to follow, and headed in the direction of the highway, so she pressed on, following the man's trail like a whitetail shot in the gut. Drops of blood and heavy boot prints continued for a few hundred yards through the woods until they were interrupted by something that wasn't made by man.

Against a growing roar in the distance of vehicles flying down the highway, likely at eighty miles an hour, the woods grew more cold and lonely. Boot prints gave way to ruts, like a pickup had ditched the pavement in favor of going off-roading. Fresh tire marks cut into the dirt to signal a vehicle long gone. The man had escaped, but he'd left his warning, and she'd sent one of her own.

She stood at the edge of the road and overlooked the road ahead. Someone out there was scared of her, scared enough to send a gunman to stop her. Before she'd even had a chance to show what she could bring to the competition, something was trying to stop her. The woods rustled at her back, urging her to abandon the fight before it had a chance to get started. They were familiar, just like the warmth of her mom's embrace, and she already missed the life she was leaving behind. But there was no choice to be made. Justice could be hers with a single bullet, and such a fate was too good to pass up, even if she had to risk her life. It wasn't just poverty or wanting her dad out from behind bars, the competition was a chance to put her life back on track. Right then and there, she made a promise to herself.

"I've got one shot," she whispered to the trees. "I won't come back until I win."

The pines didn't answer, nor did the yaupon brush

and greenbrier. The birds ignored her sincerity, and the locusts screeched over her. The dull swell of the highway, a ribbon of asphalt stretching out into an endless sky, drifted away until there was nothing left. She was met only with silence, heavy with the weight of her own demands, yet welcome all the same. Waiting in the silence was the opportunity she'd waited so long for, and she'd be damned if anything stood in her way now. Phoebe's family was counting on her, and so was her own future.

All she had to do now was reach out and take it.

Chapter 5

A man's trophies are more than proof of his accomplishments, they are perfect ornaments for an ego in need, ready to be peacocked around at a moment's notice, and even better if strung up on the wall for all to see.

Most men liked their trophies laced in gold and sparkling in the light, worth thousands of dollars, and only available to those with wallets big enough to claim it for themselves. If gold wasn't an option, diamonds would have to do. For those who thought themselves better than worldly riches, they sought trophies on a screen. A climbing number on an account bestowed on them by people with more.

Butler was no such man. He preferred his trophies to have once sucked in the earth's oxygen for themselves. He preferred them mounted and displayed. He preferred them dead. Those were the ones he was most proud of. There were plenty more in the house his antics had purchased him, historical artifacts ranging from revolutionary muskets to the infamous Amnesty

Colt wielded by the gunslinger Butch Cassidy. There were stolen jewels, sacks of gold, pictures, and documents aged beyond recognition, all telling the most outlandish tales throughout the country's history that he loved so much.

He had the fortune of being able to spend as much as he wanted during his globetrotting, and considering he was a man who didn't care for the pomp and circumstance of the big city, his humble five-hundred-acre property north of Austin suited him just nicely. It afforded him his own gun range right out in the backyard, and a home large enough to hold every trophy he could manage to get his hands on. Those twenty-foot ceilings in just about every room had come in handy, especially throughout the last few years.

At the heart of his home was the one room he treasured the most. Visitors would deem it a trophy room, but it was so much more to him. It was his entire lifetime's conquest, reaching up into the air like a cathedral made of dark oak and brass, filled with a unique mixture of leather, taxidermy chemicals, and ash from a fireplace that never saw enough cold nights. There wasn't a single place the human eye could focus that didn't muster a story that ended in blood.

Butler found himself standing at the center of his pride and joy. His boots were planted on top of a bearskin rug, a reminder of his trip to Montana, where an eight-hundred-pound grizzly charged him head-on for thirty yards. Its pelt was beneath his feet now, and its head hung near the fireplace, jaws open and eyes locked on him just like when the bear was trying to rip his own heart out. He allowed himself yet another walkthrough of the room, his eyes scanning glass cases filled with rusty revolvers and faded pictures.

In his right hand, resting over his shoulder like a sleeping toddler, was the weapon he'd used to build an empire in his own name, to carve out a legacy for himself. It was old, its wood polished but scarred beyond recognition, its barrel worn down and still fighting against surface rust every day it had to face the Texas humidity. It wasn't flashy like the custom pieces in his collection, but it was the one that had started it all. He ran his fingers along the stock, feeling the familiar grooves, the weight that had become an extension of his arm. This rifle had been with him since he was a boy, squirrel hunting in the piney woods back east. It had been with him through every hardship life could ever throw at him, and it had carried him through to find riches and fame he couldn't have imagined for himself. It was every bit as accurate as the day he first held it, arguably more so now.

As he perused his own collection of antiquities adorned by trophies slayed by his own hand, he allowed his mind to wander to every impossible shot he'd made. He thought of the whitetail in Colorado that earned him a record-breaking 214-5/8 score through the Boone and Crockett system, and the five hundred yards that separated the rifle from the buck, five times the distance of the lethal range of the bullet. He thought of the mountain lion struck down in Arizona midair after leaping from a cliff in a lethal attack on his camera crew. He thought of the wild boar in Oklahoma that no one even believed existed until Butler sent a bullet through its eye at two hundred and fifty yards.

Each trophy was more than a decoration, it was a story, a legacy that he'd carefully crafted and documented through the years. His fans weren't just casual viewers, they were witnesses to what shouldn't be possible, day in and day out.

His mind finally went back to the shot that started it all. Back then, he was filming himself with a phone clipped to his chest. It was in the Sandia Mountains of New Mexico, where he was given a rare opportunity to hunt the Rocky Mountain bighorn sheep that were still being reintroduced to the area. It was part conservation, part trophy hunt, but it was the first time he was able to use footage to make a living.

He could still feel the brisk air that filled his lungs that morning, the warmth of the sunrise hitting his face as he stared up a mountain he couldn't dare to climb. What he saw at the top of those mountains was unlike anything he'd ever laid eyes on before. It was a coyote, nipping and hollering at the sheep nearly twice its size, hundreds of yards up a near-vertical cliff. The coyote was chasing it to the other side of the mountain, and in a moment of either sheer stupidity or genius, Butler did the only thing that came to mind, he lifted the rifle and fired a warning shot in the direction of the two beasts, hoping to free his target to be tracked down.

It would become known as the impossible lob shot of Sandia, and it would cement his name in the history books for generations to come. Instead of the warning shot sailing over the mountain and falling harmlessly on the other side, the shot pushed the sheep over the crest just in time for the bullet to fall from the sky and penetrate its spinal column, killing it instantly. What came after that footage was released had become a blur, but it led him to stardom, and he never looked back. He'd turned those shots into fame, into sponsorships, into a life he never imagined back when he was a troublemaking kid stealing credit in the woods.

He stopped at the far wall, a massive display of rifles and pistols rising like an arsenal for a military force through time. He reached up to the top shelf, empty and waiting, and hung the old rifle on its hanger. No plaque, no name, just the wood and steel gleaming in the firelight. It looked out of place among the legends, unnamed and mysterious, but it was the heart of his collection.

The rifle had built his empire. It was capable of things no one should be able to do, he'd come to know that through the years, even if he lacked the spine needed to come clean about it. Defying physics wasn't out of the question, and that made for an interesting influencer, personality, and wannabe actor. People wanted to see ricocheted shots, unheard of distances, unthinkable targets. He just gave them what they wanted. The rifle never missed, not once.

As soon as the rifle was returned to its place in his trophy room, his phone buzzed in his pocket. It was an unwelcome distraction from the peace he found surrounded by his prized possessions. He pulled it out, the screen lighting his face with a corporate logo he'd seen enough of for a thousand lifetimes. One of his sponsors, a big oil tycoon with deep pockets and deeper demands. Butler answered, leaning against the display case.

"Butler, you there?" the voice barked, thick with Texas drawl and entitlement.

"Yes, sir," he answered.

"I been meanin' to get ahold of you after that dadgum video you posted. You got everyone more riled up than a coyote in a chicken coop. You know I ain't gonna tell you how to do your job, but—"

"But you're gonna go ahead and tell me how to do my job, right?"

"Just listen," the voice urged. "This competition, the *Texas Sure Shot,* it ain't what you think it is. We've already worked out a deal ahead of time. It ain't a game, ya hear me? That executive order ain't meant for everyone."

"What does that mean?"

"It means you can't lose."

"I never intended to."

"You win that order and give a good ol' speech that'll give everyone the warm fuzzy feelin' in their stomachs they want so much. You don't tell anyone what you'll use it for. If you have to, say it will be used for charity work. People love that shit."

Butler did everything he could to fight back the sigh that he wanted to let out so desperately. All he could do was nod.

"I'll take the silence as a yes."

"Sure," he finally said.

"Good. The executive order is fancy politician talk for a favor. So, you go out there and win us that favor so we use it to push some things through on our end. The less you know, the better. You hear me? You gotta win, boy. No excuses."

Butler's jaw tightened. "Yes, sir."

He knew deep down that it didn't really matter how many trophies adorned his wall, or how large his lifetime earnings would become. The empire he built wasn't truly his, not as long as he had to answer to so many other people. Ultimately, he was at the beck and call of those who owned him, those who wrote his checks. All he had to do was smile for the cameras.

One day, he hoped, he could answer to someone other than faceless sponsors and amorphous companies. It was times like this when no trophy on the wall could compare to having someone, anyone, to stand beside him. He was alone, in all of his fame and fortune, and that was just something he'd have to get used to.

He glanced back up at the rifle he'd just placed on the wall as he jammed his thumb on the red button to end the phone call. The same rifle that had delivered his empire was the one thing he couldn't stand to think about when these feelings swirled up in him again. He stared endlessly, lost in a spiral of his own making. That rifle was a steward to a life that wasn't his to live, a testament to a legacy that wasn't his to wield, but more than that, it was a reminder.

When the money was all gone, the home was taken, and an empire crumbled to the ground, nothing would change the fact that the rifle was not his. He'd used it to the best of his abilities, and he'd made something out of himself because of it, but when it was all said and done, it belonged to someone else. It was the property of a different family, the heirloom of a girl he could never forget.

He turned to leave the trophy room before her name came to mind again. He didn't want another sleepless night thinking about what had become of her. He would do anything to change what happened, or at least that's what he told himself on those nights lying in bed staring at the ceiling. He knew that wasn't true though, because he still kept it for himself.

When his hand touched the doorknob, he looked

back one more time at the rifle hanging silently at the other end of the room, and the memory of her face, the sinking realization he may never see her again, and the way she looked back at him before he turned to leave came rushing back. There was something inside him that was broken, and all he had to do was pretend it wasn't for just a little longer. He had to lie to himself one more time.

He missed Phoebe.

Chapter 6

Hitchhiking is a lost art.

Or maybe it's just a rightfully dead hallmark of a time long gone, a time where people could trust a stranger for something as simple as a ride without asking for something in return. Most people wouldn't be caught dead putting their thumb up on the highway, waiting on a driver to pull over so they could toss everything they own into the back seat of someone they had never met before. Others might daydream about the freedom it could offer, or the tales they could tell from a lifetime of traveling.

On the other hand, not many people think about what it's like to pick up a stranger and invite them into your own vehicle. There's as much risk in letting someone slide into the passenger seat as there is in the person doing the hitchhiking. You never know what people have going on in their heads, and you certainly can't tell ahead of time which ones are capable of causing harm.

Regardless of these rather glaringly obvious facts

of life, there is one rule that everyone can agree on. You probably shouldn't pull over and let someone into your car if they are carrying a rifle down the highway.

Phoebe didn't care about that, she only cared about one thing—getting to Austin.

Phoebe stood at the road's edge, her boots cracked and dusty, the heat rising in waves that made the horizon dance. Her Remington was slung over her shoulder like a warning she didn't need to voice. The duffel at her feet was a sad sack of survival items, including a flannel stiff with old sweat, a pocketknife worn to a nub, crumpled bills mixed with .22 rounds that were worth more than gold in her world. She'd walked miles from the woods where the man had tried to buy her silence, her thumb out for hours, trucks thundering past with drivers who saw the rifle and sped up, or slowed to leer.

All she needed was one to stop. Her luck dwindled down to almost nothing, until a rusted semi with a cab that stank of cheap cigarettes and even cheaper whiskey crawled next to where she was walking. The driver's eyes narrowed at the gun before flicking to her face.

"Goin' far?"

The door swung open, but Phoebe said nothing. She tossed her duffel in the back and climbed in, the Remington resting across her lap, barrel pointed at the floorboard but always ready. The driver eased on the gas pedal and began shifting through what seemed like dozens of gears in order to get the rig up to speed. It was quiet at first, something Phoebe could appreciate. As the miles dragged on, the radio spat static and snippets of the competition through local news.

Even though Phoebe was quite content leaving the

radio as the only sound in the cabin, the driver finally summoned the courage to look over at her and open his mouth. He spoke through a mustache that blended into an unkempt beard littered with crumbs of a donut he'd had hours before.

"Why you out here by yourself?"

"Tryin' to get to Austin," she answered, trying to keep her response short.

"You're in luck," he said.

A few minutes of silence crept back between them, but the driver was determined to spark a conversation worth having.

"My name's Rusty…" His voice trailed off as a hint to Phoebe.

"Annie," she lied.

"Well, little Annie, I sure am glad I came through when I did. Funny story, all things considered. I had a flat a couple hundred miles back that put me behind schedule. 'Cause of that, I gotta drive a little later tonight, but it'll put me goin' through Austin at almost dinner time."

This time, Phoebe wouldn't oblige his hint. She knew what he was getting at, and she was having none of it.

"That's nice," she said, looking out the passenger window, trying not to give him too much attention.

"Yes, ma'am. Gets lonely out here, you know?"

"No, I don't, to be honest."

"I bet you don't, lookin' like that."

This time, Phoebe ignored him. Her gut was twisting, and she was beginning to regret climbing into the passenger seat of a stranger. Her fingers gripped the wooden stock of her Remington a little tighter, even though she knew the consequences of using it all too well. They'd take her away, put her in a jail right next to her dad, and they'd never see the light of day.

She was in between a rock and a hard place, and all she could do was hope things wouldn't take a turn for the worst.

Rusty must've started to feel the tension setting in between them, because he allowed silence to return for the next hour. He hummed patiently as they drove down the highway at a steady seventy-five miles an hour. It wasn't long before the familiar skyline of the capital of Texas began to come into view.

It had been years since Phoebe laid eyes on the city of Austin. It was growing like a storm on the horizon, and her chest tightened a little more with every mile they grew closer to its center.

"You got somewhere you need me to drop you off, hunny?"

Phoebe sighed at the last word to escape from Rusty's lips, taking the time to think about her answer.

"Metro Park," she stated calmly.

"Ahh, the old Butler park." He chuckled. "It's just around the corner, actually."

Despite his innocence, the name fell on Phoebe like an anvil in an old cartoon. The breath was knocked out of her lungs, her thoughts spiraled into oblivion, and she was left reeling, trying to put herself together after the mere mention of the name Butler. It would be a few more minutes before Phoebe could gather her breath, and her courage, to speak up again.

"This'll do," she said, reaching down to grab her duffel.

The rig hissed and squeaked as Rusty brought it to a slow crawl. It stopped with a violent shake before he reached down to kill the diesel motor that had groaned and complained their entire trip. The cabin had a different kind of feeling without the endless rumbling and roaring that sent them careening down the highway. It was eerie.

Phoebe reached for the door handle, her boots already itching for solid ground. She moved with haste, but still tried to hide her uneasiness so as not to stir Rusty up. She knew better than to trust a man with her back turned.

"Hold up, darlin'," he said, interrupting her escape and sending her stomach sinking down to the muddy floorboard. "It ain't every day I haul a girl with a long gun and legs for days like you. I'd say a coupla hours ride is at least worth thirty minutes in the back, wouldn't you?"

"No," she said firmly, still refusing to make eye contact with him.

"You don't think I deserve just a little gratitude for goin' outta my way for you?"

"You have my gratitude, now let me out."

"I don't got nothin', baby." Rusty chuckled, low and wet, and reached over to grab Phoebe's thigh before she could say otherwise. His meaty fingers digging into her muscle as she tensed up.

"I said let me out."

"I got a nice comfy bed in the back, curtains that close, and I even got a couple hundred bucks tucked away for such an occasion if you need a little extra motivation to get you all riled up and ready."

This time, Phoebe turned her deadly gaze to Rusty. "Let go."

"Make me." He didn't hesitate.

So Phoebe did just that. Against a backdrop of

distant laughter, tunes from a fiddle, and the commotion of a festival soon to be, a fight broke out.

The butt of the Remington met Rusty's chin with enough force to cause his teeth to clatter in his skull like dice in a cup. He was dazed, but not for long.

Phoebe ripped open the door handle and fell out of the eighteen-wheeler, smacking her shoulder against the pavement and sending her belongings scattering around her. Before she could get to her feet again, Rusty was already bearing down on her, his mouth bloody and his eyes furious.

"You think you're better than me? Hitchin' with that peashooter, actin' all tough." He yanked her close, dragging her across the concrete, his breath hot and rank. "You're about to find out what tough really feels like." He shifted his weight to try and pin her. He pushed her against the passenger door of the rig with one hand and let his other go free, roaming her body against her will. The world narrowed down to the stink of him and the fire exploding in her gut. Time shattered, the way it did when a trigger kissed the breaking point. The Remington was lying a few feet away, useless out of her grasp. All she could do was fight back.

She twisted, driving her forehead into his nose, the crunch of cartilage sharp and violent. Blood sprayed from Rusty's nose, splashing Phoebe across the face and almost blinding her in the process.

He roared in anger, his face a mask of blood and fury. "I'll kill you, bitch!" His fist swung wild like a hammer aimed at her skull. Phoebe rolled out of the way, the concrete biting her palms as she dove for the old .22 rifle still lying on the ground, waiting to be used by any means necessary.

She could see the realization hit Rusty like he was being struck by his own eighteen-wheeler when he saw her pop up with the Remington pushed to her shoulder, aimed right at his torso. She locked the bolt into place, chambering a single round with a gliding flick of metal on metal.

Rusty spat a wad of blood out on the concrete. "Go on then, shoot me. See what happens."

Her finger curled, pressure mounting, her father's words a thunder in her ears. One squeeze, and he'd drop, the .22 bullet bouncing around in his chest like a pissed off wasp, blood blooming dark on his shirt, his eyes going vacant like the game she'd dressed a lifetime ago. It would be simple. She'd call it self-defense, a necessity in a world that didn't care about her. She had it all planned out, and she had all the rage boiling in her gut needed to squeeze the trigger. She'd killed for less, for food, for survival, but this was a man, and the line was thin, the fall eternal.

She exhaled, then eased off. Not here. Not now.

When he saw Phoebe's mercy overtake her, he mistook it for weakness and charged with a bellow. His fists were raised high into the air like clubs, but his bloodied nose had left his vision as nothing but a blur.

Phoebe sidestepped, then hurled the stock of the Remington around until it connected with the back of Rusty's head with a spine-tingling crack. He crumpled to the ground, but he was a sturdy man and refused to back down. From his belly, he lunged up, grabbing her leg, yanking her down. Gravel scraped her back as they rolled, his weight crushing, his bloodied face inches from hers, spitting curses. She kneed his groin, the impact a dull thud, and finally was able to roll on top of her attacker, straddling him, squeezing his ribs with her knees.

The next few seconds were fueled only by red-hot rage. She lifted the Remington high into the air and waited just long enough for Rusty to realize what was happening to him. Then, she brought it down with every ounce of strength she could muster.

The stock smashed his jaw, sending teeth flying from his bloodied and swollen mouth. He couldn't fight back, he could barely defend himself, but Phoebe didn't stop. She brought the stock up into the air, then slammed it down again, and again, and again. She didn't stop until Rusty collapsed onto the concrete, alive but just barely.

Phoebe rose, allowing the tunnel vision soaked in red to finally begin to relent. Her breath was ragged as she gathered her meager belongings off the concrete. With everything she owned slung across her back, she turned to face the Butler Metro Park in downtown Austin, where hopefully, her and her family's life would be changed forever.

THE *TEXAS SURE Shot* competition was already being brought to life. Tents sprawled across the park like a frontier town being reborn beneath the skyscrapers, chuckwagons belched thick hickory and mesquite smoke, and banners whipped overhead in the breeze. A crowd was already forming as occasional pops of fairground pellet guns fired off in celebration. It was a spectacle, raw and untamed, and it sent Phoebe's heart into a different kind of anxiousness.

This was the beginning. If she could win this thing,

her father could walk free, but if she lost, she'd have nothing to show for it. She couldn't shake the feeling that her whole life had come down to this one event, this one opportunity bestowed by a governor she didn't know.

She walked into the park, pushing her way through a mess of cowboys, carnies, and families doing their best to keep up with their kids already covered in cotton candy. Phones glowed without end. Someone whooped and then fired off what sounded like a .44 magnum bullet into the air as the crowd jeered and cheered in response. Phoebe ignored them all and walked toward the registration tent like she owned the place.

The man sitting at the desk looked like a radio host of the 1930s. A delicately stitched pearl snap and starched jeans with boots that most likely cost more than she'd ever seen in her lifetime waited for her to step forward. He eyed her battered .22 before saying a single word with the kind of drawl that belonged in an old black-and-white western movie.

"Name?"

"Phoebe Anne," she said as she scribbled on a clipboard and then handed it back.

The stamp fell like a gavel, and her fate was sealed, just in time for the announcer's voice to boom over the speakers. It was warm and folksy, and for reasons she couldn't explain, brought her right back to her childhood. She embraced the beginning of the *Texas Sure Shot* like it had already given her everything she needed in life. It was the first time she felt secure in who she was, in who she'd become, since before her dad was taken. The voice carried on, listing names like a graduation ceremony to deafening cheers by the crowd growing by the second.

She couldn't see who was on the stage from where she was standing, but she could see a massive projector screen showing the faces of contestants eager to put their name in the ring. The announcer read each of them without missing a beat, and Phoebe could see their faces light up when called. Some gave a reassuring wave, others flexed or did gimmicks to make the crowd laugh. Phoebe was content hanging out in the back of the crowd, waiting on her name to be said without so much as a slight recognition of herself.

"And don't forget the hitchhiker who just taught a trucker the meaning of Texas manners," the announcer hollered.

Phoebe's hair stood up straight. She didn't realize anyone had seen what happened, much less the entire crowd. Then, she saw her face on the screen, and her cheeks turned bright red.

"Phoebe Anne!"

The crowd cheered, and those standing around her gave her plenty of pats on the back, but Phoebe's world had just turned upside down. Instead of celebrating with the people of Austin, instead of soaking in the moment where she could finally get her life back on track, all she could do was hear that announcer say her name over and over again in her head. That voice was familiar, like she'd heard it a lifetime ago, and when she finally figured out who it was, her heart exploded like a 12-gauge birdshot, tearing apart a paper target.

It was Butler.

Chapter 7

Repressed memories can be a funny thing.

These aren't necessarily funny in a laughing out loud with your buddies kind of way, more so in an unthinkable, life-shattering kind of way. Sometimes they can be so far down in the subconscious that even the brain doing all the repressing is surprised at how easily they can be freed to unleash havoc.

The name Butler had just uttered was ricocheting through the hollows of his own skull, tearing a hole in every lie he'd told himself through the years, sending him in a dizzying spiral that felt impossible to escape from. It didn't help that he was standing in front of a crowd of what had to be thousands of people, and holding a microphone in his hand, exaggerating every frail breath he tried to take. He stood frozen on the stage, the microphone a dead weight in his hand, the crowd's roar fading to a dull throb behind his eyes.

The lights were too bright in his eyes, the air too thick in his lungs, the whole festival suddenly felt like a trap he couldn't break free from. It was the first time he'd said her name out loud since they'd parted, and the moment those two words moved past his lips, his world tilted, and the past came crashing in like a flood through a busted dam.

He didn't see Phoebe as she stood in front of him today. He saw her at twelve years old, her head tilted on the stock of that all-too-familiar rifle, eyes wide open as she lined up her sights on a target no kid her age should be able to hit. He saw her face when she came out of the trees to find the cops hauling her father away in their back seat. He saw her push the Winchester at his chest before turning to face down a life she didn't deserve.

"*Take this,*" she told him that day so long ago. They had fully intended to meet later that day, or maybe even the next morning, so that she could get her family's heirloom rifle back. That never happened, though.

Instead of thinking about what Phoebe had endured for so many years, about what she had gone through having to grow up without her father, he thought only of what that old Winchester had given him since she placed the rifle in his hands. He thought of the Sandia Lob Shot and how it catapulted him into stardom. Then, he thought of what she might've had for dinner the night before.

Despite his popularity, the platform he'd been given as the host of the first-ever *Texas Sure Shot* competition, he'd done nothing but bring his life around full circle. There she was, walking across the stage like a ghost coming to collect a toll he didn't have.

The planks under his boots felt like they were sinking, the stage a ship taking on water, the crowd's faces blurring into a sea of judgment. She'd looked right through him, no spark, no hate, just nothing. She walked away without a word, her stride saying she'd survived worse than him. If he was being honest with himself, he wasn't even sure if she remembered him. The look she gave him was empty, like maybe she'd forgotten everything.

He had no choice but to move on, even if he felt like he was hovering above his own body, staring down with pity at his own misfortune. He cried out another name into the mic that sat heavy like lead in his fist, his grin a mask cracking at the edges, his eyes subverting a drastic meltdown.

Phoebe Anne.

The name looped over and over. It was stuck in his head like a jammed round in the barrel of a gun, and he was afraid of what he might think when it finally came free. He'd searched for her, or at least that's what he told himself. Quiet drives through old towns, scrolling forgotten forums, asking questions to no one in particular. He told himself that she'd just vanished, that she didn't want to see him, and he believed his own lies. So much so that he'd convinced himself it was better off if they never came face to face again. Deep down, he knew what he really believed, though. He needed that Winchester.

He shouted another name, and the crowd cheered again. His eyes shot down to the newly elected governor sitting in the front row, clapping mindlessly through a smile that was all teeth. He wore a silver-belly felt cowboy hat tipped back on his head, his legs were crossed, and his pants rode high enough to show-case his ostrich leather boots. Governor Frank Rourke was the man behind it all, the man pulling the strings. That made him the man responsible for bringing Butler face-to-face with his own misdeeds.

The *Texas Sure Shot* was given to Butler by the governor. It was his latest crowning achievement, but now it felt more like a cage. He wanted to bolt offstage and not stop until he reached the trophy room he loved so much, the one place where he could bury himself in the past that had been so good to him. He wanted to run from the girl who'd taught him everything, from the rifle that chose her, from the guilt that gnawed on his guts.

"Folks," he rasped into the microphone at last, voice steady by grit alone, eyes locked on Phoebe in the crowd even though she wouldn't even look in his direction. "The *Texas Sure Shot* is more than just a competition. It's a testament to who we are as Texans, our culture, our values, and what we can give to the United States of America, and the world."

This time, the governor himself led the cheerful response with a whistle that could be heard all the way in Washington. It wasn't enough to break Butler's increasingly awkward gaze locked onto Phoebe, but it was enough to keep him talking.

"We all know the grand prize, a once-in-a-lifetime opportunity granted by the governor himself." Butler gestured to the man in the cowboy hat who had already taken the political opportunity to face the crowd, and the cameras, with a delightful wave and beaming smile. "It'll give the winner a chance to ask a favor from the great state of Texas, anything they could think of, within reason, of course." Butler gave a wink that was half directed at Phoebe's passing glance and the crowd hanging on his every word.

"What you don't know is what it'll take to win that favor," he continued. "These aren't just trick shots that old Buffalo Bill could pull off in the 1800s. These will test the very best modern shooters, push them to their limits, and force them to challenge the laws of physics and nature. And when I say them, I mean myself too!"

Butler closed his eyes, trying his best to give the crowd their moment to show enthusiasm for his own entry into the competition, but all he could think about was Phoebe. Even behind his own eyelids, he could see her. He opened them again, just in time to see her staring back at him.

"The *Texas Sure Shot* will be a one-of-a-kind experience to behold from a thousand yards out, from the top of a speeding train, from sunrise to sunset, from places you could never see coming. It isn't about showing off what's already been done, it's about showcasing what could never be pulled off. We've put together the few shooters who think they have what it takes, but they're about to find out this ain't gonna be no picnic!"

The crowd roared as the governor nodded in approval. Butler overlooked the people gathered to witness the beginnings of what was meant to be a historical event. It was supposed to be one of the greatest feats of shooting prowess to ever be on display, and he was meant to be its headliner. All he could think about was the fact that his empire was built on smoke, and she was the fire. Phoebe was the real star, but he didn't know if he had what it took to let the world know. As he stared at the smiling faces, he knew they were there for him, but he also knew it was all a lie.

The grand prize, the governor's executive order, was nothing more than a scheme worked out behind closed doors between the people who signed his checks and the people who would write the law for the next four years.

Butler's voice droned on into the microphone, not even he could pay attention to what he was prompted to read. The crowd hung on every word, too. All Butler could truly focus on was her.

She stood there, arms crossed, the Remington a quiet threat at her side, her gaze distinctly avoiding his own. The spiral he was trapped in tightened, guilt coiled like smoke in his chest.

Butler was beside himself. He was caught between the ones who owned him and the one he owed everything to. It was an inescapable weight bearing down on him more and more by the second. He stood on that stage with a lump in his throat and his stomach twisting in knots. He couldn't bring himself to look away from her, even though she was doing everything possible to not look at him.

Another swell of the crowd tried to lull him back into reality, but it was swallowed by the memory of that Winchester still hanging on his wall. The whisper of that rifle all the way back in his trophy room was louder than this crowd could ever manage to be. It was more than wood and steel. It was fate itself, trying desperately to speak to him, to right the wrongs of his path, the ones he was trying too hard to cling to. The urge to flee was a physical ache, his boots itching to carry him offstage, sprinting anywhere but the middle of Butler Metro Park. He could disappear, let the sponsors rage into the void, and the competition burn to the ground. But the lights held him, the crowd chained him, and Phoebe's presence was quickly becoming a bullet he knew he couldn't dodge.

The governor stood to accommodate the crowd

once more, cameras flashed, and people responded in kind. It was a picture-perfect moment, punctuated by a surprise Butler didn't see coming. Governor Frank's ostrich boots hit the stage like a gavel, and the band struck up a brassy rendition of "Deep in the Heart of Texas." Butler's mouth kept moving, words tumbling out on autopilot, something about honor and heritage as an introduction to the man who had won an election of a lifetime, but Butler's eyes stayed locked onto Phoebe. She hadn't moved. She stared past him, past the governor, past the whole damn circus, into some middle distance only she could see.

A ripple suddenly moved through the front rows. It was the kind of movement that Butler would have noticed in a heartbeat if it had happened in the middle of the woods, or across the plains as the sun came down over the horizon. A black windbreaker and a black cap weren't enough to draw attention, but the man's hand jammed into the jacket pocket should have been. He snapped toward the stage in the peripherals of Butler's vision, still not enough to snap his focus on Phoebe. His pocket bulged, his arm twitched, and the crowd's cheers rose to mask it all, thanks to the governor's grandstanding.

Phoebe finally moved. It wasn't much, but it was enough to send Butler hurtling back into reality, just in time to realize he was already a half-second too late.

That half-second was all the capped man needed. He shoved forward, elbowing a teenage girl aside. His hand yanked free of the pocket. Sunlight glinted off blued steel, revealing a snub-nosed .38, hammer already locked back. His arm rose in a stiff, practiced arc, muzzle tracking the governor's waving hand. The band hit the final chorus. The crowd surged, oblivious to the horrors of what was about to unfold. The gunman vaulted the railing, boots skidding on sawdust.

Fifteen yards away.

Ten.

Five.

His gunman's finger whitened on the trigger just as a woman let out the kind of scream that keeps men up at night. Her voice sliced the music in half, and the festival dissolved into chaos.

Chapter 8

The Fastest Man with a Gun Who Ever Lived is the title bestowed upon a man named Bob Munden, who set worldwide records with a quick draw that clocked in at an unbelievable two-tenths of a second.

It's the kind of speed the myth of the West tried to capture, the kind of legend that is so far-fetched it is nearly impossible to deem real. But it could not be denied. It's the kind of speed that makes the phrase *in the blink of an eye* the complete truth. When it came time for Bob Munden to draw his revolver, the only people who were able to witness his quick draw were the ones who didn't blink when it happened. Everyone else was left only to their imaginations.

This is the kind of speed Phoebe was capable of, even if she never really had the chance to showcase it for others to see. This was her chance, and she didn't come all this way to hold back. Nothing was going to stop her from taking advantage of the opportunity right at her feet, not even a stranger determined to gun down the one man capable of granting her a life-changing pardon. She didn't hesitate to do what she needed to do.

Phoebe was already closing the distance, one boot in front of the other as her fingers wrapped around the walnut grip of the little .22 that was clearly in over its head. Most would call the rifle useless at such a distance, against such a target.

The gunman had already shoved through the front row, and even though no one else at the event was able to pick up on what was happening, she was already getting ready to put a stop to it. She saw the bulge twitch, saw the way his shoulders squared, saw the cold focus in eyes shaded by a ball cap pulled low. She knew the look. She'd seen it in coyotes circling their prey back home, in drunks who thought the rent that kept a roof over her and her mom's head was optional, in every shadow that had ever tried to take what was hers. He was fifteen feet from the stage when he produced his revolver, aiming it right at Governor Frank Rourke, who was mid-wave, ostrich boots planted wide, silver-belly hat tipped back, grinning like a man who owned the sky.

The gunman's arm started to rise, fabric stretching tight over the shape of a snub-nose. He was quick, but not as quick as Phoebe. She jammed the rifle into her shoulder before the gunman could curl his finger around the trigger, and in the blink of an eye, their lives were changed forever.

A firing pin struck the .22 bullet with a single squeeze of the trigger. The crack of the shot was small, almost polite, lost in the sound of chaos that had already started to unfold, but it was more than enough.

The bullet took the gunman in the meat of his right hand, dead center between the second and third knuckles. Its impact snapped his wrist backward, sending the snub-nosed revolver scattering to the floor. The gunman's scream came out high and ragged, a sound more animal than human. His knees buckled. Blood poured between his fingers as he clutched the ruin of his hand. The index finger dangled by a thread of skin and tendon, twitching relentlessly as the blood continued to spray out.

The crowd inhaled as one, a single, stunned gasp that sucked the air from the park. Phoebe stood ten feet away, boots planted, rifle steady as a fence post in a raging summer thunderstorm. Smoke curled from the barrel in a lazy spiral as she watched the gunman fold in on himself, knees hitting the dirt, blood pooling dark and glossy all around him.

Butler was already moving, vaulting the rail, boots pounding against the pavement, shoulder driving into the gunman's ribs before the man could think to reach for the dropped pistol with his left hand. Security swarmed next, three polo-shirted rent-a-cops piling on in an effort to save their own jobs after failing to do the one thing they were being paid to do. They slapped zip-ties tight around his wrists in an instant, and every second of it was caught on the projector screen. Whoever was controlling the camera captured the gunman's draw, the shot, the finger nearly severed, the blood arcing in a perfect crescent before splattering across a little boy's cowboy hat two rows back. Then it slowly panned over before freezing on Phoebe's face.

The crowd detonated in response, starting in the back with a low rumble like thunder in the distance before what looked like hundreds of phones shot up into the air. Tiny screens flashed against the sun, some with blinding lights, others frantically searching the park to get Phoebe on camera.

Then something unimaginable happened, starting with a single voice cutting through the chaos, raw and eager.

"Sure shot!"

That voice was joined by a few others, then a few dozen others, before what sounded like hundreds of people chanting over and over and over again, drowning out the pleas for help from the man still bleeding on the ground.

"Sure shot! Sure shot!"

Governor Rourke was standing on the stage, frozen in place, hat still tipped too far back, mouth half-open. His eyes flicked from the bleeding gunman to Phoebe and back again, like he was trying to decide if he'd just been saved or sentenced. Then he started clapping, slow, deliberate claps that cracked through the noise like gunshots of their own. The crowd followed.

Hats sailed into the air. A beer bottle exploded against the stage. Someone started stomping on the bleachers, a drumbeat that shook Phoebe's vision as she tried to take in what was happening all around her. The chant swelled, becoming a living thing with teeth and claws that could never hope to be stopped.

"SURE SHOT! SURE SHOT! SURE SHOT!"

Phoebe felt it hit her chest like a physical blow. The name wasn't hers just yet, but it wrapped around her like a brand, searing itself into every fiber of her being. She lowered the .22, letting the end of the barrel fall to the ground, and watched as the man she couldn't bring herself to speak to was the first to jump into action.

Butler was off the stage in a heartbeat and lost in the cheering crowd. He hauled the gunman to his feet, blood dripping from the man's chin, his good eye wild with pain and shock. The severed finger lay in the concrete in a puddle of blood, and for a split second, Phoebe could've sworn she saw it twitch.

She stood in the eye of the storm, absorbing everything as her boots stayed rooted into the dirt and her heart hammered against her ribs. The crowd pressed closer, a tide of faces and phones and flashing cameras. Someone reached out to touch her sleeve. She shrugged them off without looking.

Governor Rourke bounded down the steps right behind Butler, but instead of going after the man who just tried to assassinate him in cold blood, he locked eyes with Phoebe and approached her. He grabbed her hand without saying a word and pumped it like he was trying to strike oil.

"Thank you," he whispered closely before changing his demeanor to face the crowd. "Give it up for this young lady!" His voice boomed even without a microphone. "She just saved the whole damn state!"

Phoebe's first thought was to yank her hand free. She never was one to enjoy being touched by anyone, much less a stranger. The governor just wanted to parade her around after what she'd done. "I saved you," she said, just loud enough for only the two of them to hear. "Don't make it more than it is."

The governor's grin faltered for a heartbeat, but he recovered quicker than Phoebe had been able to squeeze the trigger on her rifle, turning back to the crowd with arms raised like he'd orchestrated the whole thing.

Phoebe pulled away, stepping back into the endless

swirl of bodies and noise. The chant didn't miss a beat. If anything, it grew louder, hungrier, feeding on the blood spilled by her hand and the continued howls of pain from the would-be shooter. She needed air, to get away from the eyes that felt like hands crawling over her skin. It didn't matter that hundreds of people were chanting her name over and over again. She just had to get away for a while.

Phoebe pushed through the crowd, shoulder-checking a man who tried to film her face up close. His phone clattered to the ground, but he didn't even notice or care enough to stop yelling in chorus with the rest of them. She kept moving, boots crunching over spilled popcorn and crushed cups, until she broke free near the chuckwagon line bellowing smoke into the air. The smell of brisket and beans hit her like a wall, grounding her for a second.

Her hands shook from the adrenaline dump that always came after taking a shot at another human in public. That was something most people would get arrested for. This time, she'd been hailed as a hero by the governor of the state of Texas. So much had happened to her in a matter of hours, it was hard to take in.

She leaned her rifle against a hay bale and flexed her fingers, watching the blood rush back into them. The rifle looked small now, almost toy-like, but it had done its job. It had also turned her into a spectacle, however. Someone with their name on hundreds of lips before she'd even fired her first official round in the competition. Phoebe wiped sweat from her brow with the back of her sleeve, making it impossible to see the shadow that crossed the hay bale in that split second.

A figure twelve inches taller than her, with arms

built like two separate tree trunks, loomed behind where Phoebe was trying her best to hide. It took longer than she would've liked to notice him standing behind her, but when she whipped around, all she could feel was relief that it wasn't Butler.

His name was Brad Kremer, he was former military, something Phoebe really only knew since he was introduced earlier as Sergeant Kremer. The crowd seemed to know him well, judging by how loud they responded to hearing his name. Phoebe had heard there were shooters from every walk of life, so it didn't come as a surprise that the army would be well represented.

Brad stood over Phoebe, propped up on one prosthetic leg that clicked like a metronome everywhere he walked. It didn't seem to faze him a bit, but that might've also been due to the fact that he was double fisting beers. He pushed one out to Phoebe with a half-hearted smile.

"Hell of an opening act you got there," he said.

Phoebe didn't drink, she never really had, but she reached for the beer anyway. "Didn't plan on it."

"You better take advantage," he told her between a chug of the bottle remaining in his left hand. "You're what they call a crowd favorite, through and through."

"Thanks," she responded. "I think."

"Name's Brad—"

"Kremer," she cut him off. "I was paying attention."

"Looks like it. You'll forgive me for not knowin' your name. Too busy roundin' these up." He lifted his drink.

"Phoebe."

"Well, Phoebe, let me be the first to genuinely

welcome you to the competition. Just so you know, all of us are meetin' up here in a little bit down at the bar. Governor won't be there, just us gunslingers." He gave her a wink.

"Thanks for the warnin'," she said, adding a smirk before taking a swig of beer and immediately regretting it as the bitterness filled her mouth. She forced it down anyway and did nothing to hide her disgust, warranting a chuckle from Brad.

An awkward silence fell over them, one that Phoebe was unwilling to break. She just wanted to be left alone, but peace and quiet were for the life she once had. It would escape her as long as she was a part of this competition. Brad tried one more time to spark a conversation, but even he struggled to say anything meaningful.

"I'd ask your claim to fame, but I think you just showed everyone why you should be around."

"Am I supposed to ask about yours?" she shot back, trying to deflect one more time.

"Just doin' my job is all."

"So humble," she said before stopping herself from nervously taking another swig.

"You ever shot somethin' more than twenty-five hundred yards away?" This time, Brad didn't have an ounce of humility in his voice, it was pure competition.

"Can't say I have."

Brad turned to walk away, leaving Phoebe to ponder what she was getting into and just how hard the competition was going to be. But Brad was the kind of man who never let anyone else have the last word, and he let her have it with his back turned.

"Trust me, it ain't easy," he called out without facing her. "Even harder when the guy's movin'!"

He limped off into the haze of floodlights kicking on as the sun began its descent, leaving Phoebe alone with the sizzle of meat on the pit and the distant roar that hadn't let up. She glanced down at the bottle in her hand and thought better of drinking anymore, choosing to toss it in the closest blue trash can. She slung the rifle back over her shoulder and made her way into the crowd that was still chanting her newest nickname over and over and over again.

It followed her everywhere she went at the park like a stray dog. As soon as someone could see her face, they would shout *Sure Shot* at her like it was the greatest compliment she'd ever be graced with. She couldn't escape it. Drunk cowboys hanging on cattle panels, kids waving their arms frantically, clusters of girls in the same pair of tall white cowboy boots, all had something to say as soon as they saw her.

She ignored them all.

When she found the pop gun target range, she allowed herself to stop and soak in the familiarity of staring down a few targets. When she glanced down at the rifle fixated on a swivel, she noticed they weren't pop guns at all. They were lasers backed by speakers that played the same sound of a gunshot about six times before another sound of a shotgun pump rang out. The mismatch of the toy rifle and the pump shotgun sounds gave Phoebe a real reason to chuckle.

"Most people don't notice," a grizzled old man caught wind of her amusement and interrupted her once again.

He wore an apron with a tag on the front, labeling himself as the range master. His mustache swept across either side of his face like a broom, and his hat brim was pulled low over his eyes. He chewed tobacco slowly, spitting a stream into the dirt with a smack of his lips before he decided to speak up again.

"Knew you'd sniff your way here," he rasped. "That little peashooter just made you a target bigger than this whole damned city. Hope you're ready for that."

"I've been through worse."

The old man cackled, a sound like dry leaves in the wind, blowing across concrete. "I can hear Annie Oakley's rifle whispering from here. Can't you?"

Phoebe's hand tightened on the stock of the toy rifle as she locked eyes with the old man. How could he know? It only took a few seconds for Phoebe to decide that the old man didn't know anything, that he was just rambling, and she had no reason to take him seriously.

"Don't ignore it," he leaned in and told her quietly. "She's calling."

With those final words, the old range master tipped his hat and vanished into a tent. Phoebe half expected him to pop out laughing like it was all a joke, but he was gone, leaving her to consider what had just happened in silence. She stood alone, the chant swelling again as the event turned from a welcome ceremony to an alcohol-fueled party.

The crowd found her again, surging from the main path like a flash flood bearing down on her in a few seconds. Phones aimed at her face, blinding her with flashing lights as random people shouted questions at her. A woman thrust a baby at her for a photo. A skeevy man tried to drape an arm around her shoulders nonchalantly. She shoved through, head down, until the noise crested into a single, roaring wave. They weren't cheering the save, Phoebe knew it as much as they did. They were cheering the blood, the disembodied finger writhing in the concrete, the instinct deep down inside her to be the first to squeeze the trigger when no one else could.

"Sure Shot! Sure Shot! Sure Shot!"

Chapter 9

The Bucket of Bullets was more than a watering hole for the less-than-charming shooters of the Sure Shot competition—it was a powder keg waiting to blow.

They called it a saloon, but when Phoebe brushed beyond the barely lifted canvas flap of the tent, she was met with a sweat-soaked fever dream reeking of sour mash, cheap cigarette smoke, and the stench of men going too many days without a shower. It was framed with old cedar beams just strong enough to keep the canvas tarp standing, along with a few lanterns strung around seemingly at random. They cast golden light across angry faces and half-empty tumblers of whiskey.

It looked like a scene out of an old western film without a cell phone in sight, all except for the flatscreen television hanging ominously in the corner like it had been dragged in from the future to change the lives of every drunken mess loitering around.

Phoebe's boots were silent as she entered, hitting only sawdust scattered around the floor. It masked her entry enough to not draw every eye in the tented saloon. The first thing that hit her wasn't the smell or the sheer amount of strange faces, it was the noise, a rattle of cackling, boasting, and hollering. Clinking of bottles and glasses punctuated each voice with an unforgettable tinge.

She knew that when it came down to it, she didn't belong in such a place, not really, but the crowd just outside was already ready to crown her and she needed to see who else was in the running to take what she needed so desperately for herself. She needed to know if there was a single soul getting drunk in the saloon who'd be willing to put their life on the line for that grand prize, because she was.

She edged along the bar that was nothing more than a long plank of oak polished by a thousand elbows, and shouted for water to a bartender whose mustache looked like it had been glued on by a blind man. He slid the room-temperature bottle across without a word. Phoebe leaned into the shadows, eyes scanning the room the way she'd scan the tree line back home for coyotes. The shooters were circled around tables or standing around without anything to lean on, each one a different breed of predator. She counted them, measuring the distance between friendship and a bullet just in case worst came to worst.

Brad Kremer stood first in her sights, propped against a support post like he'd grown there. The military veteran was as tall as a pine, lean as a whip, and didn't seem to be bothered by much at all. His prosthetic leg caught the lantern light, reflecting off a twisted combination of titanium and carbon fiber. It was a war souvenir that clicked softly when he shifted weight, promising a million stories that would never be spoken aloud. Brad didn't talk much, just nursed a bottle of water of his own and watched the room with eyes that had seen too many bloody days. He wore a faded, curled-up camo cap pulled low, the brim frayed just like the look in his eyes.

Phoebe nodded once. He nodded back.

At the next table over, a woman sat like a queen on a throne, surrounded by drunk men trying to get her attention. She was in her early twenties, judging from the makeup and the attire she deemed appropriate to wear in such a place. Even though Phoebe didn't know who she was, the men barking at her sure did. They said her name over and over, like they couldn't get enough of it—Lena Mitchell. She carried a stainless steel six-shooter on her hip and seemed content to just bask in the attention of every passerby, even though she refused to answer any of their questions. It took only a few minutes of listening to determine that this woman had found fame online, and only a few more minutes to find out she was the daughter of an even more famous competition shooter.

Phoebe sighed at the misfortune of having to compete against someone like Lena, took a sip of her water, and continued scanning the crowd.

This time, it was the bartender who caught her attention. Through his thinly veiled mustache, he hollered a name that couldn't be forgotten. Plinky. It was the kind of name that had to be a title, a nickname earned, not given. The man who answered the call looked like he belonged to a generation born a hundred and fifty years ago. His beard nearly touched his stomach and had become bleached white through the years, matching the stringy, thinning hair that reached down his back.

The old man prattled on and on to the bartender,

who had heard it all before. Plinky claimed to be a direct descendant of exhibition shooters of the real Wild West, says his ancestors were the original endurance shooters, who could keep a two-inch spread across tens of thousands of bullets fired across days and days and days. He carried a couple of ancient Colts covered in surface rust like they hadn't been used since Taft took over Teddy's position at the head of the table.

"Most people think it's all about the gun," he croaked to the bartender, who had completely checked out by now. "It's the wind. It lies. You just have to listen closer to hear the truth."

Phoebe scoffed and took another drink. Not everyone in the Bucket of Bullets saloon was a competition shooter. There were plenty of women preying on those who didn't know any better, men who fancied themselves shooters and only wanted to pretend to be among the greatest, and those who had no business being there other than the fact that they were being paid to attend. Phoebe knew what a man on payroll looked like, whether it was for security, spying, or a combination—they were standing around, blending in as best they could.

The barrel of a rifle carried by a man in need of a haircut slammed into one of the lanterns hanging from a beam, sending golden light spiraling in a dizzying pace throughout the saloon. Drunks groaned at the man's clumsiness, and the bartender hollered a threat that shouldn't be said in public.

There was only one person with the brains needed to stand up on his chair, reach up to the top of the tent, and grab hold of the lantern to prevent it from swinging. He was the kind of man who never missed a meal, who smiled when you made eye contact with him, who radiated warmth even in a room full of cold-blooded killers. He didn't carry a gun on him as far as Phoebe could see. His actions were met with applause from pretty much everyone else, and the man certainly didn't mind the attention.

"Three cheers for Juan Marquez!" one man screamed out.

"Shut up!" another man shouted him down.

Juan took a bow while standing on top of the chair still then waved his hand with a grin before sitting down without saying a word.

Phoebe tried her best to make a mental note of his face. Men like him, kind and inviting on the surface, had a way of sneaking up on you when you least expected it. She didn't know anything about his qualifications, but she knew he was a competitor in the truest sense.

By the time he had planted his ass back down into the chair, there was only one person left who demanded all the attention in the room. He was making rounds like he was the owner of the place, shaking hands and patting shoulders like it was his money that organized the entire event. Phoebe slunk back behind another table to avoid him for a few more minutes, just to give her the time to judge him before coming face to face. He did the same thing to every person he met, he approached with a shit-eating-grin, hand extended for a quick shake, then he leaned in close and said something before introducing himself as Mr. Will Randy Hearst.

Phoebe watched him go to Plinky first, a mistake honest enough for anyone to make. Mr. Hearst didn't know Plinky was a talker, but he put two and two together in a hurry. The old man Plinky was already getting started on a story that likely had no ending when Will patted his shoulder gently, turned, and walked away without another word.

He wore a suit as crisp as a new hundred-dollar bill, donned a smile as sharp as a skinning knife. He carried a gold-plated revolver sunk deep into a black leather holster hung on the outside of his hip. His eyes were black and emotionless despite what he was trying to sell those he was introducing himself to. They reflected nothing and absorbed everything. He raised his glass to the table in front of her and toasted them behind a thinly veiled lie about how steep the competition appeared to be.

When he finally turned his attention to Phoebe at the back of the tent, his grin widened until it became indistinguishable from a fissure opening the earth itself to the depths of hell. He was sweaty, pale, and his eyes were sharper than ever. He had a sinister look up close, and it sent a shiver down Phoebe's spine. This man was made of pure evil, she just knew it.

"Will Randy Hearst," he said with his hand outstretched. "And you're the hero of the hour. Phoebe, isn't it? Quite the entrance."

Phoebe didn't take his hand. She glanced down at it, then back at his eyes, and nodded.

"Just doin' what needed doing."

Hearst withdrew his hand, unfazed, and leaned against the bar like he owned it.

"Humble. I like that."

Phoebe didn't answer, hoping the silence would drive him away. It didn't.

He leaned in close, choosing not to pat her on the shoulder, but whispered into her ear anyway. "When I win—and I will win—I'm going to request the great state of Texas to change the world from the inside out, through and through. I just don't want you to get your hopes up too much, is all."

When he returned to an appropriate distance between them, he smiled as big as he could, stretching his lips out across his face in the hopes that Phoebe would return the favor in kind. She didn't.

"I look forward to seein' you out there," he told her. "Just so you know, it's gonna be a little bit harder than shooting a six foot two hundred pound man fifteen yards away."

Phoebe lifted her water to him, trying to urge him to leave her alone as gently as possible. Her eyes crossed with Brad's first who was watching her from behind Will. She broke eye contact with him only when she noticed the one who was drawing all the eyes in the room.

Butler had entered the Bucket of Bullets, and with that, all of her anxiousness, stress, and worry gave way to a sinking sense of uneasiness that sent her thoughts hurtling back to the woods she grew up in. She thought of the way he looked at her, the way he used to make jokes about what their life would be like when they grew up, the way he would always find a way to come out on top, even when it meant she'd have to settle for next in line.

They didn't speak even though their gaze was locked on one another. It was like they were sharing in their own nostalgia, waxing poetic, reminiscing about what could have been without sharing a single word. Phoebe could only guess what Butler was thinking, but she knew it was no different than hers. It was a burning yearn for an idea of one another that didn't exist, quenched by the unfortunate reality of what they had become, of what life had done to them. They were only children when they had grown close to each other, but they weren't those people anymore, and neither of them knew exactly how such a stark fact should be addressed. The only thing they could do was hope the other would figure it out first.

As luck would have it, they would both be saved by a literal bell. Someone suddenly started clanging an old steel bell like it was dinnertime, but instead of watching people come running in, they did the opposite.

Phoebe watched as most of the drunks inside the tent were instantly sober enough to stand in unison, set their drinks down, and form a line to exit the saloon. The bartender disappeared, the dull roar of passing conversation punctuated by bellows of laughter or shouts of anger gave way to silence, the clattering of bottles turned into the shuffling of boots. Within a few uncomfortable minutes, the tent was cleared out, leaving only a handful of people standing around as clueless as ever.

Lit only by the glow of lanterns hanging still in the tent, there stood seven contestants forced to come to terms with who they would be up against. Will Randy Hearst, Brad Kremer, Plinky, Lena Mitchell, and Juan Marquez stood between Phoebe and Butler. They stared at each other, judging everything from the clothes they wore to the look in their eyes, facing down what was sure to become the most important competition in their lives. Just before the silence would become too much to bear, the television flickered to life, and the tent was filled with the bravado of the newly elected Governor Rourke in a video call.

"You'll accept my deepest apologies for not bein' there to tell y'all in person," he started, declining to wait on all of the participants in the competition to gather around. "Politics waits for no man, I'm sure you understand. However, I would like to take this moment to sincerely thank each and every one of you for putting your reputation on the line by agreeing to take part in the first-ever *Texas Sure Shot* competition."

Governor Rourke wasted no time in getting right to the point of their gathering. "You're here because you're the best of the best, there ain't a single doubt about that. You are also here because you're the best Texas has to offer. You seven are gonna show the world that if anyone's gonna mess with Texas, they're gonna have to go through the likes of y'all. You might not understand what that means just yet, but trust me, you will."

This time, his words warranted an exchange of strange glances from the shooters in the tent. Phoebe did her best not to look at Butler, but she couldn't help it. They hid the slightest smirk between them, then turned their focus back to the television, almost like they hadn't been separated for most of their adult life.

"Here's how this whole shindig is gonna play out," the governor began his explanation. "Over the next week, there's gonna be five rounds of intense, impossible shots that you're gonna have to make, and they're only gonna get harder as it goes on. Tomorrow, you're gonna be facing down a thousand-yard shot through the eye of a needle, but that's not the hard part. The only ones who will qualify to advance to the next round are the ones who strike the target—the edge of a Bowie knife made right here in the heart of Texas—and split their bullet in half. You give me both halves of a bullet, and I'll give you one more shot in the competition. Simple as that. For now, you'll wanna keep your focus on the first round, what we're callin' *The Knife Edge*."

Phoebe's first reaction was dire panic. Her .22 had no chance of making a thousand-yard shot like that, much less splitting the bullet in half on the edge of a blade. Her heart tightened, and her thoughts returned to the few memories she had of her father. They always ended with seeing him being dragged away in the back seat of a patrol car. While she spiraled, the governor just kept going like nothing had happened.

"I ain't gonna spoil the rest of the competition just so you can get a head start, but I will say that you need to prepare to achieve what most believe cannot be done by man, wielding nothing but gunpowder and lead. If you're standin' still while shootin', you better believe that target will be movin'. If you're tryin' to hit one target, you better believe there's another waiting that'll be even harder. It's gonna be a trial by fire out there, this is the only warnin' you're gonna get."

The governor let his words sink in for just a little while before he cleared his throat and started up again. "Now let's talk about the reason you're all actually here, that executive order. You know, there have been hundreds and hundreds of these things signed since Texas gave up her independence and joined the United States of America. They've all been administrative, business as usual, to help keep the train rollin' along. Well, those voters sent me to the Capitol to do somethin' different, so that's what's gonna happen. You hear me?"

While the shooters nodded as one, the governor made his point. "You're not just gonna show the world what'll happen if you mess with Texas, you're gonna show them what we're capable of when you stay outta our way."

The television clicked off just as Governor Rourke finished uttering his last word. It left Phoebe reeling. She was unsure if they'd just watched a prerecorded video or a livestream, but she did know one thing, it was going to be impossible to be too careful about who she got involved with during the competition. The stakes for her were clear—either get her dad out of prison here and now, or spend the rest of her life trying to make up for her failure to take advantage of the opportunity. As she looked around at those who would be standing in her way, a simple, inescapable fact became too obvious to ignore.

The real target was on the back of every person in the Bucket of Bullets.

Chapter 10

The Colt might've tamed the Wild West more than a century ago, but it had been unleashed upon the world once again for the first day of the *Texas Sure Shot* festival.

The morning sun hit the fairgrounds like a red-hot branding iron pressed against fresh hide, turning the swirling dust into a haze of gold and grit and hope for a tomorrow that was better than the day that came before. Chucks for breakfast were already coming off the smoker, tents were being staked, sun tea was brewing, and horses were coming off the trailer in preparation for the first of the events set to kick off soon. It was the kind of morning that cowhands dreamed of on their days off.

The itinerary was posted on bulletins like wanted posters, making sure every spectator knew exactly what was in store for the day. Vendors would be open by nine in the morning, bronc busting and team roping by eleven, bull riding by noon, just after brisket was served, then the competition would kick off before ending with a grand fireworks display celebrating the first day. There would be western poets and storytellers, reenactors, craftsmen, ranches and farms, livestock judging teams, pit masters, and those who just loved the history of the state available throughout the day for fans and families to make the event an all-day spectacle.

It was early when Phoebe stepped off the chuckwagon that had served as overnight lodging for the broke and the stubborn, and the heat slapped her awake better than any cowboy coffee boiling over an open flame ever could. The *Texas Sure Shot* competition grounds had exploded overnight. What had been a half-erected carnival the day before at the Butler Metro Park was now a full-blown Wild West fever dream on the outskirts of town. Red-and-white striped tents, brass bands sawing away at "Yellow Rose of Texas," the smell of mesquite and hickory smoke curling up from pits turned the air itself into a reflection of the culture of the Lone Star State.

She passed a group of FFA kids donning matching blue jackets, giggling at one another until they noticed Phoebe and quietened down until she passed by. There were more bearded men than she ever thought could be gathered in a single place already showing up to the event, families would be coming in next, and then the teenagers later. Soon, it would be a picturesque, postcard-worthy depiction of those who called Texas home.

She passed beneath a banner stretched across a fifty-foot-wide path that read *1ST ANNUAL TEXAS SURE SHOT*, and she knew she was right where she needed to be. The rifle slung over her shoulder felt small and honest in a place as bizarre as this. Everywhere she looked, she saw remnants of a past that seemed to only exist in movies and textbooks. Vendors were hawking their wares to anyone passing by, a mechanical bull shaped like a longhorn snorted steam and bucked beneath a sign that ironically titled the monstrosity as *THE EXECUTIVE ORDER.* She passed a taqueria and michelada stand where the cashier wore a sash reading *MISS IMPOSSIBLE SHOT 2025*, and kept moving until the crowd noise thinned and the shooting lanes came into view at the backside of the fairgrounds.

They had built the first round on a stretch of prairie south of the loop, a thousand-yard ribbon of packed caliche flanked by bleachers that rose like cliffs on either side, never extending out beyond the firing line that had already been painted.

At the closest end stood the coveted shooters' benches. They were nothing more than seven islands of scarred oak beneath a canvas awning, but they sat waiting like Olympic podiums, destined to platform the true winner. At the other end—further than most people could see with their naked eye—rested a single Bowie knife glinting in the sunlight, propped upright in a block of oak. Between them rested a steel hoop the size of the top of a Coke can, dead center in the lane. Split the bullet on the knife and walk away with both halves to the next round of the competition, or miss and go home. It would be as simple as that.

The brass band in the distance began to strike up "Deep in the Heart of Texas" as Phoebe stood there visualizing a world where she could win it all. It would start here, with her taking a seat at the shooter's bench, squeezing the trigger, and watching the Bowie knife slice her bullet in half. Soon, the range would be crowded with spectators, dignitaries, and contestants alike, but for now, it was just Phoebe and the edge of a knife over a thousand yards away.

She patted the stock of her rifle, knowing it didn't stand a chance at making the shot that was requested of them. There wasn't much she could do about that. Her thoughts quickly went back to the Winchester that should have been in her hands. She thought about how unfair life had been to put her in a situation where the one thing that could ensure her victory would be nowhere around. As much as she felt desperation sinking in about just how far her underpowered Remington .22 would take her, she knew there was no choice. With a sigh, she turned to go back to the fairgrounds to find something to eat.

THE NEXT FEW hours saw Phoebe nursing a plate of smoked chuck and roasted corn, given to her by a man who had seen her little display of shooting prowess back at the park. It took longer for her to take selfies and sign autographs than it did to get a plate of food, but even she would be lying if she said she didn't find enjoyment in the kindness of people who were fans of what she could do. It was something she hadn't really experienced in her life, even from her own family.

Living at the cabin with her mom didn't afford her a chance to make many friends or to meet pretty much anyone who shared a genuine interest in the things she loved. It wasn't just shooting that was bringing these people together, it was a sense of community, a respect for the past that gave them their livelihoods today. Because of that, Phoebe was able to find herself among people who thought just like she did, and even though she admittedly loved the barbecue she was holding, she truly found comfort in the fact that her world was becoming larger than the patch of trees she'd known for so long.

Her tour through the fairgrounds came to an end quicker than she would have liked. Right when she'd made the decision to splurge on a cup of sweet tea larger than any she'd ever held before. It took two hands to take a sip, and she was maybe the happiest she'd ever been while holding it, waiting for the competition to start. The announcer's voice cut through the crowd that had seemingly quadrupled in size since earlier that morning, static hissing through the air just long enough to catch everyone's attention.

"The first-ever *Texas Sure Shot* competition is set to begin in thirty minutes. Contestants, please make your way to the range where you will be assigned a lane to take your shot. Fans, grab a seat while you still can."

Just like that, Phoebe's casual demeanor turned ice cold. She was lost in a sea of excitement, her stomach twisting in knots like she was being tied up to a hitching post by her intestines. She was just another face in the crowd, but there was something in her that couldn't be found in anyone else at the festival. Now it was time to showcase what she had kept hidden from the world for so long.

By the time she had returned to the lanes, it was like a completely different world. What was once some empty benches surrounded by even emptier bleachers was now nothing more than a pit of early drinking fanatics screaming until their faces turned red, backed by the rise and fall of a live band churning their way through just about every country song that barely mentioned the state of Texas. The familiar twang of "Luckenbach, Texas," gave way to the billionth airing of "God Blessed Texas," and the crowd somehow went even wilder.

Phoebe took in the overwhelming scene like a gladiator about to face death itself in the arena. It was unlike anything she'd ever laid eyes on before. She couldn't stop herself from being stunned at what she'd gotten herself into, and the only thing that snapped her back to reality was the fact that she was already the last shooter to find her designated bench in the middle of all the chaos.

A bearded man checked her identification amid a return of chants with her newly labeled nickname, then another man with an even longer beard pointed her to the only open lane at the range. She was the only shooter who wasn't basking in the warm welcome of the swarming fans literally hooting and hollering as loud as they possibly could. She felt like she was the latest attraction in a zoo, not at all like she'd just entered the fight she'd waited most of her life to take on in order to free her dad.

While Phoebe did her best to take her place at lane six of seven, she allowed herself to gauge what she should be doing by glancing at her competition. Brad Kremer, the marine with a past he didn't like to talk about, was ready to go at lane one, checking elevation and distances through a handheld scope she'd never seen before. Lena Mitchell was in the middle of a live stream, holding her phone up as high as her arm would allow while twirling in circles, flashing her stainless six-gun for her viewers. Plinky leaned against the bench like it had taken all of his energy to even walk to the range. Phoebe wondered if he had the energy to keep up as the competition went on before she noticed Juan Marquez next to Plinky, waving to the crowd from lane five before pulling out all the stops with a random backflip that sent fans into a tizzy.

At the final lane of the shooting range was Butler.

He wore sponsor patches like he raced cars for a living. Remington was written across the chest like it was put there with a branding iron, Leupold traced down one sleeve, Magpul down the other. A Texas flag the size of a napkin was sewn to his shoulder in the exact spot he'd soon nestle the butt of the rifle when taking his first shot. That's when she noticed that the rifle across his arms was hers.

Phoebe felt it the way you feel a missing tooth with your tongue. Same barrel, same crescent butt plate, same faint scratch on the left-hand side that brought back memories of her dad chewing her out for it while trying to teach her to shoot at the bottom of her breath. Her heart fell through her guts until it landed on the dirt at her feet. She tasted iron at the back of her throat. She'd bitten the inside of her cheek without noticing.

The announcer—a radio voice equivalent of a ten-gallon hat—came through a megaphone amplified by modern technology, interrupting her spiraling thoughts. "Ladies and gentlemen, welcome to the inaugural *Texas Sure Shot*! Seven shooters. One knife. One thousand yards!" The crowd roared. Fireworks popped overhead even though they were lost in the sunlight as soon as they exploded.

The next voice was different, more familiar. "I want y'all to remember, this is all because of you, the voters!" The governor's voice came through the speakers, shushing the crowd as if they were bearing witness to history itself in the making. "Every shot of gunpowder-fueled freedom that takes place here is because of *you* and what you bestowed to the great Lone Star State by puttin' my ass in that chair! So, I want all of you to sit back and relax the Texas way, as the finest shooters we've ever known take the stage."

Phoebe felt like time had sped up, like she couldn't pay attention to everything going on around her at once. It was a blur. The governor's voice rattled on and on for what felt like hours, even if it only came up to about fifteen minutes. He talked up his own importance, as politicians are so keen to do, before moving on to just the kind of grit needed to win the competition and earn a favor from a man like him. He gave a history lesson on Texas-based ingenuity, on how they are pushing the boundaries of economic prosperity, on how the future depends on leadership only they can offer. He claimed the *Texas Sure Shot* competition would be studied by historians as a shining example of what small government and big thinking could achieve.

"Remember, the rules are simple." The announcer stepped back up to the forefront, forcing Phoebe to come to terms with the competition kicking off. "You can use any gun that uses powder and lead, any caliber, any bullet. For this round, though, you only get one shot. It ain't the *Texas Sure Shots* competition. Just one chance to advance and show the world you got what it takes. First up is the veteran sharpshooter and real-life American hero, Sergeant Brad Kremer!"

She joined the crowd of people watching as Brad stepped up to his shooter's bench. He didn't wave, or smile, or pay anyone a shred of attention. He simply laid down his .300 Win Mag rifle on the rest, adjusted the sandbag, and stared down the scope like it owed him money. The windsock at the 500-yard mark danced left to right. Brad waited until it hung limp, a time that found thousands of people packed around the range, all holding their breath at the same time. Phoebe felt the seconds drag on as Brad trained the sights on the edge of a blade so far away it couldn't be seen. Silence fell over the crowd long enough for the first bullet to be fired in the shooting competition to come as a surprise.

The bullet rolled across the pasture like slow thunder. Downrange, the spotter was doing his job. It took an agonizing few seconds before the bullet struck home and the spotter held up two fingers—both halves needed were accounted for. There was a projection screen at the shooters' backs, and the festival didn't explode with applause until they saw the green flag waving in the spotter's hands. The crowd gave him the kind of respectful roar that a soldier earns but never asks for. Brad racked the bolt, caught the brass, and stepped back like he'd just done something as simple as mailing a letter.

Lena Mitchell bounced forward, all sequins and stainless steel. She finally saw fit to holster the six-shooter she'd been posing with and produced a .308 that was far from picture-ready. For the first time, Phoebe felt like she was finally seeing the real Lena get to work. She moved with graceful confidence, jamming a round into the barrel and leaning her cheek down on the stock in one motion. Where Brad took forever to line up his shot, Lena fired hers before the crowd had a chance to fall silent.

This time, the cheers came like waves, crashing onto Phoebe the second another green flag was lifted into the air by the spotter. Lena had already pulled her phone out again and was spinning in circles, showing her online fans the crowd celebrating her moving onto the next round.

Phoebe suddenly felt ill. Her knees began to tremble as imposter syndrome began to set in. She was surrounded by people who did this for a living. She did it out of necessity. Her world had gotten bigger than she could've ever imagined, faster than she thought was ever possible. It was going so smoothly for everyone so far, she couldn't allow herself to fold before she had a chance to get going.

Old Plinky was next. The announcer rambled on like he was giving an ad for a radio before television existed. He was drowned out by the fans to the point where they had to increase the volume on the speakers. The band continued to play on and on as the announcer listened to himself ramble into the megaphone. Meanwhile, Plinky shuffled up to the shooter's bench, muttering about the wind while he jammed a .270 round into a rifle that had to be older than him.

Phoebe watched as he grunted and complained while sitting down, forced one eye closed, and sat still. The crowd waited anxiously, but Plinky didn't deliver like the other two shooters. He pulled off the rifle, readjusted, and leaned his head back in, only to do it two more times. Impatience was setting in as some of the more rowdy, likely drunk fans began to make their annoyances heard.

If anyone could have seen Plinky shooting, they would've predicted the outcome. He fumbled for the trigger before he was sighted in, closed both eyes, and squeezed the trigger. It recoiled hard, forcing him back a few inches in his seat as the gunshot echoed downrange. The spotter's red flag drooped like disappointment manifested in a piece of fabric. Plinky spat tobacco juice out of his lips and threw his hands into the air.

"Piece of shit rifle," his curse could only be heard by the shooters.

The band kicked into a solemn tune as Plinky filed out of the range, barely lifting his boots off the ground with every step, and the crowd laughed and jeered in response to the first shooter exiting the competition.

Phoebe felt the fear that she might be next rising in her gut, then forced it down again. What she was lacking in confidence, Juan Marquez more than made up for both of them. He wasn't cocky or rude, but he was damn sure of himself.

He produced a rattlesnake-skinned .308 AR that probably cost more than Phoebe's entire homestead, gave the crowd a grin bright enough to reflect all the way to Houston, and touched off one round so casually that it looked accidental. He didn't even sit down at the bench. He shouldered the rifle, standing upright, flicked the hair trigger that was barely hung on the reset, and didn't even wait for the spotter to lift a flag before lifting the rifle up in triumphant celebration. Juan blew a kiss to the bleachers as the spotter hoisted up the familiar green flag.

Will Randy Hearst was next in line, and that meant Phoebe's shot was coming up. Nerves began to set in, and she felt her fingertips begin to tremble. It was a dizzying sensation that climbed its way up through her limbs and into every single thought that raced through her head. Anxiety swallowed her up whole while Hearst went to work with his 6.5 Creedmoor. She should've paid attention to the one who she knew tried to stop her from showing up. She should've stared him down to see what she was up against. She should have known better than to pass up a chance to see who that man really was.

Deep down, she just thought she'd have more time.

A gunshot rang out, and before Phoebe could realize what was happening, Will Randy Hearst was lifting his rifle into the air and waving at the crowd. The announcer's voice cried out over the festival once again, congratulating Hearst for being the latest to showcase a green flag from the spotter so far away. His voice droned on with rehearsed excitement, eliciting just the kind of response from the attendees that'd keep his paycheck coming.

Phoebe's boots felt full of cement by the time her name was called. Most of the shooters had already advanced, and only one had fallen short. She didn't want to be the second, she couldn't be. The chant that followed her all around the park started up once again before she could take her seat at the bench.

"Sure Shot! Sure Shot! Sure Shot!"

Their voices roared at her back, giving her momentum she couldn't find all by herself just yet. She looked down at the .22 and her chest tightened. She knew it couldn't make a thousand-yard shot, no matter how good she was. Most rimfire bullets like that would do good to hit a target a hundred yards out. Before she could put her hand around the rifle, she felt a grip on her shoulder. When she turned to see who it was, she saw a face she never expected—Brad's.

"Here," he said. "Use mine."

He pushed out his .300 Win Mag until it hit Phoebe's hands. Before she could thank him, the announcer's voice cut through the air. "Any gun, any caliber, folks!"

She didn't know what to say, and anything she could've come up with would have only been drowned out by the crowd's roar anyway. She grabbed the rifle and smiled. Brad returned a stretched-out grin of his own, then turned around and left her to work. When Phoebe sat down at the bench and shouldered a rifle she'd never shot before, she couldn't help but glance over at Butler.

The look in his eyes was something she'd never forget. He gripped her rifle tight enough to turn his knuckles white, like he wouldn't turn it over even if his own life was on the line. She had to rely on the generosity of a stranger when the man she was once best friends with refused to give up her own family heirloom rifle, the gun she should have been holding by all rights.

The moment her cheek touched the butt of the rifle, the entire world and all of her problems fell away. She wasn't thinking about the betrayal she felt from Butler or her dad still sitting behind bars. She wasn't thinking about her mom, or even the next round in the competition. Tunnel vision allowed her to see only the Bowie knife waiting a thousand yards away. Everything was foreign. The eye relief on the scope, the feeling of the stock on her skin, the scent of gunpowder lingering from the bullet Brad had fired to keep himself in the competition. She didn't trust anything but her own instinct.

Even though the knife was too far away to see and the wind was blowing too hard to trust, she knew better than to second-guess her own instincts. The scope had more hash marks than she'd ever seen, but windage and elevation distances weren't something she measured in numbers—she used her gut.

Her finger curled around the trigger just in time for the crowd to go as silent as the wind sweeping across her face, threatening to blow her hair into her eyes when she least expected it. She could hear the 500-yard windsock whipping in the distance more than she could hear a single peep out of any of the spectators. She waited until the sun's light broke through the cloud, casting a single ray down on the target waiting to split her bullet in half like a glorious beacon awaiting her arrival. She exhaled until there wasn't anything left in her lungs, then eased the trigger back, noticing it had gone cold since the last bullet, and stopped for just a second when she felt its resistance.

The recoil slamming into her shoulder caught her off guard, and for a split second, she thought she had squeezed the trigger prematurely. It was already too late to take the shot back though, all she could do was wait and see, just like everyone else at the festival. The end of the rifle burst with flames, and the bullet was unleashed. She didn't suck in any more air until she knew one way or another. It was the longest three seconds of her life. The crack of the rifle still hung in the air when the spotter was trying to make the call. Phoebe's vision had started to blur from holding her breath so long. There was a certain sense of helplessness that came between squeezing the trigger and striking the target. It was up to the hands of fate now, whether she'd be done before ever getting started, or if she had a fighting chance to free her dad. It all came down to a spotter a thousand yards away.

Just when she couldn't dare to hold her breath any longer, the green flag snapped high into the air. The bullet had kissed the knife's edge just like she'd intended. The crowd detonated, returning to their chants of the name she was truly beginning to live up to, whether she believed it or not.

"Sure Shot! Sure Shot!"

It rang out over and over again, until finally, Phoebe allowed herself to turn and take it all in. The screen overhead replayed the bullet splitting on the edge of the Bowie knife like butter. They showed it from what felt like a dozen angles, even in slow motion, and then Phoebe saw her own face. She was smiling. The camera had found its way to her, and the crowd loved every second of it. They grew louder, to the point where the announcer was forced to drop the megaphone and wait ten, twenty, thirty seconds for the crowd to finally begin to quieten down.

Phoebe's ears rang worse from the thousands of people screaming at her than from the gunshot itself. She lowered Brad's rifle like it was made of glass and set it gently on the bench. That's when she locked eyes with Butler.

He hadn't moved. Hadn't cheered. Hadn't even blinked. Her Winchester was already laid out on the bench like he was growing impatient with having to wait for her. No one else could see what Phoebe saw in Butler, but she knew that look in his eyes, she knew he was afraid of what was about to happen.

"And now, the man who needs no introduction, the king of impossible shots himself—"

The bleachers damn near lifted off their foundations, interrupting the announcer before he could get Butler's name out. Women screamed until their faces turned red. Men hurled their hats into the sky. A drone buzzed overhead, dropping red-white-and-blue streamers that caught the wind just right.

Butler didn't play to the cameras, not this time. He

simply leaned his head over until his cheek touched the stock, using the kind of reverence most folks saved for church altars. He was in a shooting position for less than a second before he squeezed the trigger, sat the rifle down, and stood up to give the crowd his trademark grin before the bullet even had a chance to find the edge of the blade.

The knife flashed once, a silver wink against the sun, and the spotter's green flag shot skyward before the echo ever reached the bleachers.

Fireworks cracked overhead once again as the crowd showed their appreciation as best they could. Butler waved like he was being paraded around against his will. He offered a gentle bow before pulling off his sunglasses just long enough to shoot a wink to where the governor was sitting. Then, he did something Phoebe would've never expected.

He turned to face her, but he didn't smile or tip his hat. He made sure she was staring right back at him, and as the band fired up the Jimmie Rodgers classic "T Is For Texas," he mouthed two words only she could read on his lips.

"I'm sorry."

Chapter 11

"If I had my way, I'd make sure every single soul in this whole damn state feared the law."

"There wouldn't be such a thing as repeat offenders, or murderers out on parole, or cop-hatin' sons of bitches takin' to the streets. Because if I really, truly had my way, their asses would be in a jail cell until it was time to stick 'em in the ground."

Hidden behind black, beady eyes, a startlingly sinister grin that could sell a shot of whiskey to a man dying of alcoholism, and a crooked finger pointed at anyone who would lend a passing ear—Will Randy Hearst basked in his own ego.

"Could you imagine what we could do without all these criminals gettin' turned loose on our good, law-abiding people by paid-for judges? Hell, I might even go as far as to say Texas independence could be ours once again!"

He lifted his arms, palms facing the sky, and looked up as if he was asking for help to carry out his own worst dreams from the heavens above.

"I'd throw them all in jail, and I'd never let 'em out. God can sort 'em out for all I care, we've got better things to do."

His own listeners had dwindled to the point of only being a few drunks who could no longer spare even a chuckle at his rantings, but that didn't stop him. He carried on, laying out his most dastardly ideas that would get him punched square in the nose by anyone who had a past.

The day that saw only one of the contestants exit the competition was coming to a close. Poor old Plinky didn't stand a chance with all of his ailments, and as the sun went down over the trees and night swallowed up the festival, all of the grandeur must've seemed like a punishment for his own aging. Endless fireworks popped overhead as the latest country singer produced by Nashville, who swore he was raised in Texas, strummed an acoustic guitar, only to be stifled by overpowered rock drums, electric guitars, and whatever else the label thought could redefine the genre.

Phoebe was propped up against the backside of a food truck struggling to churn out enough brisket tacos to appease the concertgoers. She listened to their chaos as the man who introduced himself as Will Randy Hearst unknowingly turned himself into her mortal enemy. Her lips curled in disgust, and her thoughts sank to depths she never thought she'd be capable of going to. Then, a curious question arose.

Did he know?

Was that why he sent some gun hand to stop her from entering the competition? What was he trying to prevent from happening? She couldn't stomach listening to him anymore, and she couldn't stand what being around him for only a few seconds was forcing her to consider. Just when she had summoned the courage to go and give that man a piece of her mind, a different voice came from behind her, and Phoebe immediately wished she could spend the night listening to Hearst's ramblings instead.

"What a nutjob, right?"

Butler had found her, and he even had the nerve to reach out and grasp her shoulder to try and get her attention. The only problem was the fact that he was about a decade too late.

Phoebe didn't turn around. She didn't need to. She'd know that voice if it came to her in a dream or a nightmare. It was the voice that kept her up at night, the one that she thought of every time their family couldn't afford groceries or to keep the lights on in their cabin, the one that left an empty promise of returning to be the final words between them.

Butler stood three feet away, his cap covered in sponsor patches still pulled low, hands shoved deep in the pockets of jeans that cost more than everything Phoebe had on. He looked like a thousand-dollar puppy in trouble for something it knew it shouldn't have done. The only problem was that there was no sympathy to be found in Phoebe. She had to fight her own thoughts begging her to hate Butler's guts.

Even though she didn't want to, Phoebe finally faced him. The colored stage lights strobed across his cheekbones, making him look like a stranger wearing the face of the boy she once cared so deeply for. It was strange looking into his eyes again. She couldn't put her finger on the feelings it stirred in her, but she knew they weren't all hatred, and that made her turn the anger inward. It had been so long, he was practically a stranger as far as she was concerned, but no matter how many times she told herself to despise Butler, she just couldn't.

"Funny," she said, "findin' you hidin' in the shadows."

"Phoebe, please let me explain." He took a step closer. "I wasn't hidin'. I was lookin' for you. I've been lookin' for you for a long ass time."

"I don't really see why you gotta lie to me now, after all these years. That's how you wanna do this?"

"I'm bein' honest."

"The hell you are, Butler." Her eyebrows sank as she dug in her heels. "You're gonna sit here and tell me you never went lookin' in the last place you saw me? You didn't even try."

"I tried for years, and then somethin' inside me said that you probably didn't even want to see my face, so I stopped lookin'."

"Well, at least you figured that part out."

"We need to—"

"No," she corrected him immediately. "There ain't no *we* anymore. It's just you, like it always was. It's you and my rifle you never gave back like you said you would."

"You don't understand."

"No, you don't, Butler. You never did. You've had everything handed to you for your whole miserable life. You ever heard of a silver spoon? It's still wedged in that lyin' mouth of yours as we speak!"

Butler's jaw flexed. "I know I can't go back in time and change everythin' that happened."

"You can change one thing," she answered him. "You can give me my rifle back. The rifle that belonged to my dad, who's still in jail, since you haven't asked."

"That's what I want to talk about."

"Yeah?" Phoebe was genuinely curious to hear his response.

She waited patiently as the music continued to thump behind them. Somewhere, a kid screamed in excitement, and another wailed in frustration. Instead of Butler's heart-spoken confession, she heard the hate-filled voice of Hearst cutting through the noise.

"They're animals! Why do they deserve the same freedom we have to work so hard for? It's costing us, which I'll have you know is no different than the state itself, and it's a detriment to the future our ancestors worked so hard to build. They deserve only to see you and I thrive behind the bars that keep them in check," Hearst ranted.

"I can't even think with that son of a bitch back there." Butler couldn't help but acknowledge what they were hearing.

Phoebe's eyes remained locked onto Butler's. She watched as the color left his face, replaced by the neon strobing lights from the concert still blaring in the background. Finally, he swallowed hard enough for her to hear the click in his throat.

"I kept it safe," he said, the words coming out strangled. "I swear I did, and I meant to give it back as soon as I was—"

"Stop," she cut him off. "I don't need to hear your excuses. If you ain't gonna give it back, then we're done here."

His eyes flicked away. He was drawn toward the dark between the trailers, toward Hearst, toward anything but her. When they came back, they were glassy with something that looked too much like fear. "I can't," he whispered.

"Can't or won't?"

He didn't answer. Just stood there with a stupid look plastered across his face like that was supposed to satisfy her.

"What aren't you tellin' me, Butler?"

He opened his mouth, closed it, then opened it again before thinking better of any words that came to mind. His head shook once, small and desperate. Hearst's voice rolled over them both again, closer now, drunk and vicious and hateful.

"And when I take that grand prize, I'm askin' the governor for one thing and one thing only." A theatrical pause, glass clinking. "An executive order that'll keep them all right where they belong. No appeals. No pardons. No nothin'. We lock the door and throw the key away."

Phoebe's blood turned to ice water in her veins. It was almost too much to bear. The disgust washed over her, and Butler knew exactly what she was feeling, even if she didn't have to say a word—Phoebe could tell as much. The only problem was, he was acting no different than Hearst. They would both let her fail to get what they want, they didn't care if her dad would sit in a cell the rest of his life or not. The best thing she could think to do was to let Butler know the truth.

"You should be talkin' to him," Phoebe said, jerking her thumb behind her to the ranting lunatic who had no idea he was making a lifetime enemy out of her. "You'd just assume to see my dad rotting in jail than do the decent thing and help to get him out. You only care about yourself, you always have, Butler."

His answer cracked out of him like he'd been holding them behind his teeth for years. "If I lose that rifle…" He stopped short of his own sentence, throat working, eyes shining wet under the lights.

"What happens if you lose, Butler?" She stepped into him until they were almost touching. "Tell me. Tell me how it's so much more important than anythin' I've got goin' on. Say it to my goddam face."

He looked at her like a man staring down the barrel of the only gun he's ever been afraid of. "I can't," he said again, raw and hoarse, like he didn't want the words to escape his mouth. "If I could trade every damn thing I own to hand it over right now, I would. But I can't. There are things bigger than me ridin' on it. People who'd come for me. For my family, for…" His jaw clamped shut so hard she heard his teeth clatter together.

Phoebe felt the distance between them stretch wider than it's ever been before. "You're scared," she said, tasting the truth of it. "You know exactly what that rifle is capable of, and that's why you won't give it back. You know because you've built a career on my family's back. My dad warned me of people like you, of what someone could do if they got their hands on a rifle that couldn't miss. You always turned red when I said I was gonna be the next Annie Oakley 'cause I had her gun, now I see why. You took advantage of me when I was just a little girl, and you haven't changed a bit."

"You have every reason to hate me." He tried to walk her down off the edge of a cliff. "I'm not sayin' you shouldn't hate everythin' about me, I'm just tryin' to ask for one more chance to prove to you."

"You've already proven who you really are. All this time, I thought you were just another greedy son of a bitch. Turns out you're just a coward wearin' the face of a man with a spine."

"Maybe I am," he rasped. "But that rifle stays with me till the last round is up. I win, I stop Hearst. I can get the order from the governor for myself and I can fix all of this. I swear on my life, I can fix this."

"No, you can't," she told him, allowing pity to enter her voice even though she hated herself for even hinting at it. "You ain't gonna fix nothin'. If you won't give me my rifle back, then you need to just get out of my way. I'll win this whole thing without it, and you'll know what it's like to be left with nothin', just like I was."

Butler went very still. The fear in his eyes turned into something hollow. Before he could answer, Phoebe went ahead and gave him another piece of her mind. "The difference between you and me is when I say I'm gonna do somethin', I actually do it."

She slammed her shoulder into his on her way out of the line for tacos that hadn't moved an inch since she started talking to Butler. It caught him off guard, but not to the point where he couldn't yell at her and try to keep explaining himself, even when Phoebe wanted nothing to do with him.

"I have a plan!" he screamed in vain. "You have to trust me! I have a plan!"

Hearst's voice rose to a fever pitch somewhere behind them, as if he was desperately trying to screech louder than Butler's voice would carry, like he knew what they were arguing about and he wanted to do his small part in making it that much worse. "And when they're all locked away forever, we'll finally have the Texas our grandaddies bled for!"

Phoebe couldn't bring herself to turn around. The

tears streaming down her face simply wouldn't allow it. She couldn't stand to face the boy she'd once known, buried beneath his own money and bad decisions. She couldn't take one more second of listening to Hearst's awful speech. She wanted to curl up alone and cry, but she didn't have that option. Her family depended on this competition, her future hung in the balance, and she couldn't let anyone stand in her way. Even if it meant she would never hold the rifle she was meant to shoot again.

She kept walking away without ever looking back, one foot in front of the other, boots crunching through the sawdust and spilled beer, fireworks exploding overhead like the world itself was coming apart at the seams.

Butler stood alone under the colored lights falling further and further behind Phoebe, still clinging to the ghost of a promise he was too afraid to keep.

Chapter 12

The first time you see two endless steel ribbons winding through the Texas landscape into the horizon can be a life-altering experience.

A rhythmic *thump thump thump* backed by the roar of a twelve-cylinder diesel engine was the kind of soundtrack that lulled travelers, explorers, businessmen, politicians, families, and anyone on the run from their own lives to sleep across an endless expanse of railway stretching out as far as the eye can see. What was once built to connect the country through innovation and grit had now become second-class in the eyes of the people who once fought tooth and nail to lay every single tie by hand.

The second round of the *Texas Sure Shot* competition came to the shooters like a fever dream. Governor Rourke explained the process like it were as simple as whipping up a batch of biscuits, even though what he was asking was nothing short of preposterous. Every person left in the competition had the same bewildered look in their eyes as the process was explained in thorough detail.

It all started with a rather lengthy backstory on a man named Captain Adam Henry Bogardus, who wasn't just a prolific shooter himself in the heyday of the Wild West, but he was also the inventor of the first glass ball trap. Modern-day skeet shooters know him as the man who started it all, but most people find Captain Bogardus to be a man lost to the pages of history. Before competition shooters were tagging steel targets hundreds of yards away or blasting clay pigeons hurled into the air, they were shooting hand-blown glass balls tossed by Captain Bogardus's own contraption. The often-ornate glass targets became known as Bogardus balls, and as luck would have it, those were the targets each shooter in the *Texas Sure Shot* competition would be facing down in the second round.

Phoebe sat in the first passenger car of the privately owned train alongside Brad Kremer, Lena Mitchell, Juan Marquez, Will Randy Hearst, and Butler, who sat at the opposite end she was at. They bounced up and down without any indication that it would come to an end, listening to the rails screech and the engine hum and the governor ramble on a television hung at the front of the car where everyone could see.

There were four other passenger cars behind them, with a restaurant car behind those and a viewing platform bringing up the rear of the train. There were more people stuffed onto those cars than what should have been legal, but with the second round of the competition having moved on board a train, there were more people who wanted to be in attendance than who could actually afford a ticket.

Phoebe glanced out of the window to her right just in time to see a pair of drones with flashing lights aimed in her direction hovering in the distance. They were live-streaming the competition for everyone at home around the world to watch. All Phoebe could do was turn away from the window and pretend they were all alone on the train.

It was her first time to ever take a ride on the railroad, even though she'd seen a million pass through town, holding up traffic and honking a horn so loud it could be heard miles away. She'd always wondered what it would be like to step foot on a train, but as the governor kept talking, she quickly began to regret having such thoughts.

Governor Rourke beamed with excitement as he laid out the rules. Each shooter would be asked to climb on top of the train as it reaches speeds of upward to thirty-five miles per hour to take their shot, but he was only just getting started. They would soon be crossing paths with another train—this one traveling in the opposite direction—equipped with one of Captain Bogardus's glass ball traps for each shooter. The goal was simple. Shoot and explode the glass ball midair and advance to the next round, or miss and go home.

The sheer amount of eye rolling and groans that came from within the passenger car full of professional shooters and one woman who was feeling more and more out of her league by the second was a sight to see. Luckily, the governor was speaking through the television again and couldn't actually witness their reactions.

The screen cut to a grainy, sepia-toned image of Captain Bogardus himself donning a mustache fit for any John Wayne western with eyes that could stare a hole through any modern man. It panned across his stoic face for a few seconds before cutting to the glass ball traps they'd be facing down. Six brass-and-steel beauties mounted on the opposing train's flatcars, each one loaded with a single crimson Bogardus ball that caught the morning sun like fresh blood swirling in a mason jar.

"One shot," the governor repeated as the television zoomed in on the target each shooter would be fixated on. "One glass ball flung from a real-life Bogardus trap doing thirty-five miles per hour the other way, facing against wind as honest as a tax man. Shatter it clean or start walkin'. We're gonna call this round *All Aboard*. Good luck, y'all."

The television clicked off, and the silence that fell over the shooters was the kind that said everything worth saying. They bounced along for a few seconds like nothing had happened, like they weren't about to climb on top of the train they were riding in and open fire on a hundred-and-fifty-year-old target thrower to explode a glass ball that was just under three inches in diameter. It was daunting and difficult to process, and Phoebe was doing the same thing every other shooter in the train was doing—trying to figure out how the hell she was going to pull it off.

Brad Kremer was the first to break the silence, but it wasn't with anything he said. He simply checked the chamber of his .300 Win Mag and spun the bolt home with a sound that somehow brought everyone back to reality.

Lena Mitchell finally put her phone down long enough to make eye contact with someone who wasn't on a screen. "So, we're basically shootin' skeet and playin' chicken at the same time, and the whole world gets to watch? Cool. Cool. Cool."

Hearst leaned back in his seat, gold-plated Colt catching the light just right, and stretched his lips out into a smile that showed a gleaming gold tooth to match his revolver. "One shot," he purred, eyes sliding to Phoebe as if she wouldn't notice. "No room for little girls and little .22s that oughta be shootin' tin cans behind a trailer. Wouldn't you feel more comfortable shootin' squirrels outta trees back at Ma and Pa's?"

Butler sat rigid at the far end of the car as Hearst mocked Phoebe relentlessly. The hard case clamped between his boots held the Winchester he wasn't supposed to have. His knuckles were bright white. He hadn't looked at Phoebe once since they'd boarded, hadn't spoken since the night before when he'd refused to do the one thing he knew he should've done long ago.

Phoebe ignored every word Hearst spoke and decided it was better to stare out the window at the pastures passing them by and the drone hovering with its flashing light blinking on and on and on. She took a few deep breaths and tried to gather her thoughts that kept threatening to return to harming Hearst in every way she could imagine. She just had to keep her focus on the reason she was here—her dad. She envisioned what it must be like to not look out a window for a decade, to wonder what happened to a family you haven't been a part of, to wish for a single opportunity that may never come.

The train whistle gave a long, mournful wail before its brakes began to hiss. A man burst through the door leading to the engine. His mustache was eerily similar to the picture they'd just seen of Captain Bogardus from almost a hundred and fifty years ago. His belly hung low, completely covering his belt buckle. He pushed his head in through the window just long enough to holler at the shooters.

"Rooftop in ninety seconds, folks! Wind is gustin' northwest at fifteen, and the roof is slick as shit, so be careful out there," he shouted. "Oh, and one more thing, the governor wanted me to tell you he wants drama, not a body count, so no dyin' out there!"

The next few minutes saw each of the shooters grab their chosen firearms—or in Phoebe's case, the only one she owned—and line up single file behind the ladder leading to the roof of the train. They were placed in the order they'd be shooting. Brad first, then Lena, Juan, Hearst, Phoebe, and finally, Butler. They climbed slowly, like they were doing so at gunpoint rather than of their own volition.

The wind hit them with enough force to send them right back down into the passenger car where they came from. When Phoebe cleared the hatch, the first thing she could see was the rolling pastures and pines with the sun still rising up in the east, casting a golden glow on the earth sprawling out in front of her. It wasn't the wind that took the breath from her lungs, it was the view.

The roof curved under her boots, slick with dew and exhaust residue that made every step feel like it could be her last. There were seven open shooting positions spread at equally distant spots on top of the passenger train car they had just climbed out of. It didn't take long to figure out that Plinky was meant to be the seventh. For a split second, Phoebe found herself wondering what the poor old man would've done trying to pull this stunt off, but she cast those thoughts aside. Each shooter had one harness that would clip to the train itself for a small security measure. As the six remaining contestants each lined up behind their spot, a handful of drones swarmed overhead, trying to capture their haunted reactions in real time for everyone to see.

Phoebe paid them no attention as she clipped her orange harness to the single steel cable running the spine of the car, dropped to one knee, and wedged her boot into a locking device that felt about as secure as a lawyer's promise. The wind whipped her hair across her eyes without remorse. She jammed it down tight behind her ears and went through the motions to check the little Remington grasped in her fingers. It was the same wood stock worn smooth from her palm, the same honest little crack when she worked the bolt that had put meat on the table more times than she could count. It felt small and plain and perfect against the madness around her.

Across the gap, the opposing train was rushing ahead in their direction, black engine belching smoke, flatcars gleaming. From Phoebe's perspective, it was like the two trains were playing chicken with one another. She braced herself for what was to come, trying her damndest to lock onto the six Bogardus traps cocked and ready to go. The glass balls inside caught the sun and flashed red, becoming beacons in the distance, getting closer and closer by the second. Her heart skipped a beat as she jammed a bullet into the chamber.

A green flare shot sky-high from the locomotive like the cruelest hands of fate had just lit the fuse. The whistle screamed one last time, and the whole world narrowed to wind and steel and the pounding of her own blood.

Brad Kremer went first. He didn't kneel, didn't flinch, just stood tall like the wind owed him money—and he was about to collect by any means necessary. The first trap sprang, sending a crimson orb shot high into the air, twisting, fighting the gusts, desperate to send it any direction but the one Brad needed. Before anyone could blink, the .300 Win Mag spoke at last, deep and final. Red mist bloomed perfectly and drifted away like a prayer cast into the heavens. Green flag. Brad advanced without so much as a nod.

Lena Mitchell was lined up next. She planted her boots wide, stainless six-gun up one-handed, phone in the other for the livestream. The trap fired, and another crimson ball launched into a high arc right above her head. She snapped a shot that looked lazy, almost bored. The orb exploded into a heart-shaped cloud that even made the drones lose their attention. She blew across the barrel like it was hot and turned her attention to the phone in her other hand.

Juan Marquez's turn was next. He grinned like this was the best day of his life, a custom assault rifle already up and ready to go at a moment's notice. The trap sprang, and the ball went higher than the rest, catching a crosswind that whipped it sideways, violently and faster than any human should be able to spot.

Boom.

The glass ball sailed on untouched, tumbling into the prairie like it was laughing at him. Red flag. Juan's grin died right there on the roof, along with any hopes he had of receiving that coveted executive order from the governor. He stood frozen for a second, but the train didn't slow for pride.

Hearst took his place slowly, his golden Colt glinting in the flickering sunlight. The trap fired without hesitation, and the ball arced high and wicked. Hearst's shot was soft, almost gentle. Glass became like bloodied snow drifting hazily across the sky. He didn't celebrate, he just turned his head and looked straight at Phoebe, lips moving slow enough to read across the wind.

"Your turn," he said with a blink-and-you'll-miss-it wink.

Phoebe's stomach flipped. The train lurched over a switch, and the harness jerked her hard enough to force the air from her lungs. Wind slammed her sideways, and she struggled to yank her own hair from her eyes in time. It was a torrent of gusts and pressure that she faced down on top of the speeding train. She fought for balance, got the .22 up, and leaned against the stock until her cheek knotted up. The trap sprang once more, and her own Bogardus ball shot up into the sky, dancing alongside the movements of the wind, unpredictable, rapid, and without warning. Phoebe tracked it as best she could for a split second, front sight wobbling, wind screaming, heart hammering so loud she felt it in her teeth. She thought of her daddy's voice and the tip he would be whispering in her ear if he were standing behind her. She breathed out until her lungs were empty, her heart was ready to skip a beat.

Pow.

The .22 bullet kissed the edge of the orb, and the whole thing detonated into a ragged red bloom that seemed to form a rose in the skies before bursting into a mist that disappeared into the breeze. Close didn't begin to cover it. Phoebe stayed kneeling, chest heaving, tasting copper and relief and terror all at once. She'd scraped by on the skin of her teeth and the grace of whatever was watching over fools, downtrodden, and piney-woods girls like her.

Last up was Butler. He hadn't moved the whole time. Just stood at the end, watching Phoebe take his spotlight one shot at a time. He dropped slowly to one knee, lifted the Winchester like it had been waiting its whole life for this moment. It's worn and familiar stock was glowing, the half-octagon and half-rounded barrel caught the sun just right. He didn't stand tall. Just stayed kneeling, stock welded to cheek, the rifle that never missed steady as it always was. His trap fired high and wild, caught a gust that should've made it impossible, before plummeting suddenly to the ground. Butler didn't even look at it. He was still locked onto Phoebe, the end of the barrel doing all the work as if it didn't even need Butler's finger to squeeze the trigger. His lips moved, but Phoebe couldn't make out what he was saying. Before she knew it, the Winchester screamed, and the ball exploded into a perfect sphere of crimson.

The trains roared past one another a fraction of an instant later, and the wind scattered what was left of the broken Bogardus balls into the atmosphere. The shooters still standing on top of the train could hear the viewing car going berserk beneath their feet. Drones swarmed in, trying to capture the reactions of the four shooters who advanced and the one who missed the mark—Juan Marquez.

Phoebe stayed on the roof long after the others started climbing down, wind drying the tears she'd never admit were there, watching the prairie roll by, indifferent as ever. Butler stopped beside her on his way to the ladder. He didn't touch her. Just stood there with the Winchester across his arms like it weighed ten thousand pounds of regret.

"I'm sorry," he said again, voice raw over the roar of the rails.

"You keep sayin' that," she answered without looking up. "You ain't sorry enough to change anythin' though, right?"

He opened his mouth—closed it—then did the only thing he could. He turned away from her without another word and followed the rest of the shooters back down the ladder into the train hurling down the tracks.

Phoebe knew he'd gone, she knew he couldn't change the past or what was driving him. She couldn't change him any more than he could change his own situation, no matter how much she wanted to. Her dad was depending on her, unable to see what she was taking on from behind bars, but she could still hope. She could still hold tight to the possibility that maybe she could change the future.

She wiped one final tear from her cheek, sucked in all of the anxiety, fear, and apprehension she was feeling, and climbed down from the top of the train to join the rest of the shooters of the competition.

Chapter 13

The locomotive was still crawling into the station, brakes hissing like an old rattlesnake that had been run over and was none too pleased about it.

The air smelled of hot iron, diesel, and the faint sweet rot of mesquite burning somewhere down the line. Butler hadn't even got both boots planted firmly on the gravel before Juan Marquez started coming completely unraveled about what had just happened to him on top of the train.

Juan was fuming mad. His face had turned beet red, drops of sweat were dribbling down his brow as his eyes turned bloodshot. He burst out of the second passenger car like hell itself had kicked him in the ass. His face had gone the color of fresh liver, eyes wild and glassy, custom AR slung across his back like he was half a heartbeat from swinging it around and turning a bad day into a massacre.

"This is bullshit!" Juan's voice cracked raw over the screech of steel on steel, over the low rumble of the crowd spilling off the viewing platform, over the muted celebration from the other shooters congratulating one another. "Absolute, complete, total bullshit! The wind caught that stupid little ball, but it didn't catch anyone else's? Mine was *rigged.* This was a trap from the start. I knew it! Everybody saw it!"

The viewing platform was already vomiting people into the station, each one adorning big hats and bigger belt buckles, their phones held high, trying to add another perspective to the commotion unfolding. Two range officers in orange vests tried to head him off. They kept their palms up and mouths moving with useless words nobody could hear over the brakes and the shouting, but Juan shoved straight through them. One stumbled hard enough to go down on one knee. Juan kept coming, boots stomping gravel like he was trying to punish every rock between him and the shooters still climbing down off the roof.

Butler was last to disembark from the train. The hard case with the Winchester hung heavy on his shoulder, heavier than it had any right to be after what he'd just done on the rooftop. The metal rungs were still warm from the sun and slick with somebody else's sweat. His palms were damp, heart knocking against his ribs like it wanted out.

His thoughts were still lingering on Phoebe's reaction, the tears streaming down her face that she didn't even mention. Phoebe had climbed down just ahead of him, the .22 rifle cradled in her arms, taking the place of her father's Winchester she yearned so desperately for. She hadn't said a word since he'd left her on the roof, hadn't even looked at him. He deserved every second of that silence. He deserved worse, and the taste in his mouth was sour with it.

Juan found the first contestant who would make

eye contact with him and exploded. Brad Kremer was the unfortunate victim, having just reached the ground. He was in the process of breaking down his .300 Win Mag with the same calm he did everything else, when Juan deemed it appropriate to get in his face. The sun hammered down, turning the dust into a haze of gold and misplaced fury. Somewhere, a cicada buzzed loud enough to cut through the shouting.

"You lose your eyes and ears with that leg, you piece of shit?" Juan got nose-to-nose with Brad, close enough that Butler could see the spit flying with every word, could smell the sour sweat and adrenaline rolling off him. "I said I want a goddamn redo! If you had any dignity, you'd be demanding a fair competition. What happened up there ain't fair, and you know it. I figured a man who'd served this country would at least understand that much."

Brad didn't even glance up. He slid the barrel into its sleeve with the same care a man might use laying a baby in a cradle. "Rules were clear. One shot. You missed."

"I didn't miss! The wind—"

"Wind was the same for all of us," Brad said, voice flat and uncaring. "You just missed. Now you go ahead and load up that tacti-cool rifle and get outta here."

Juan's fists came up white-knuckled, veins standing out on his forearms as his voice cracked with directionless anger. "Say that again, little boy."

Brad zipped the case and looked up, meeting Juan's eyes without blinking. "You missed. Simple as that."

Juan swung first. The punch landed clean on Brad's jaw, a solid meaty *thunk* that snapped his head sideways hard enough that Butler heard the pop from ten feet away. Brad didn't go down, though. Instead, he dropped the case cradling his trusty rifle and came up swinging like a man who'd gone to the depths of hell and back and lived to tell the tale. Two heartbeats later, they were on the ground—becoming an amorphous blob of fists and elbows and knees—dust exploding around them, rising into a plume of dirt and bad decisions that had no other end. Juan had a reach advantage and pure red rage on his side, but Brad had weight and the kind of muscle memory that only comes from putting your life on the line day after day for a cause that wasn't always clear, even if the job at hand was.

BUTLER SHOULD HAVE STAYED CLEAR, he should have let the range officers earn their pay and break up the scuffle that was turning into blood and broken bones in a hurry. He should have made himself scarce when all eyes were turning in the direction of the fight. Instead, he found his own eyes cutting through the growing circle of spectators—past the phones and the shouting people—until they locked right onto Phoebe.

She stood a little apart from the rest, her rifle still held easy across her body like it belonged there, hair still wild from the wind on the roof, cheeks flushed from the sun and the adrenaline rush and something else he couldn't name, something that hit him in the chest in a way he couldn't even admit to himself in the moment. She was watching the fight with an expression that wasn't anger and wasn't amusement, but instead something quieter, something strategic.

He moved before he could talk himself out of it, letting his own body take over what his thoughts couldn't help but hesitate over. Butler walked straight through the circle as people parted without being asked, and headed for the corner of the train station where no one could interrupt his conversation with the woman he wanted deep down to avoid out of his own overwhelming sense of shame.

Between him and Phoebe, there was an old man in a sweat-stained apron pouring sweet tea into mason jars faster than the crowd could drink it, ice clinking loud in the sudden hush that followed him. The smell of tea and lemon and sweat and blood mixed in the worst ways imaginable, but Butler took two jars anyway. Condensation ran cold down the glass and over his fingers, cutting through the dust and heat. He pushed onward, trying to close the gap between him and Phoebe slow enough to give him time to think of something worth saying.

THE CROWD CLOSED behind him like he'd never parted them to begin with. Brad had Juan in a headlock now, and Juan's face was turning the color of a ripe plum, his boots kicking gravel in useless circles. Blood dotted both of them, bright against the dust. Juan was throwing every kind of elbow and fist he could manage, but Brad dodged them all. With each failed attempt, Brad squeezed a little tighter around Juan's neck, trying to force him to give up the fight before it took a turn for the worse. There wasn't an ounce of submission in Juan Marquez though, the only thing he knew to do was fight back. He writhed and wriggled beneath Brad's grip before a lightbulb went off in his dimming thoughts, then he suddenly started flailing his legs to try and kick Brad's prosthetic out from underneath him. It was a cheap shot, and the crowd reacted as such, but it kept the fight going, and that was enough for Juan.

BUTLER FINALLY CAME face to face with Phoebe as the crowd swelled in response to the brutality unfolding at the train station. Her eyes flicked up, narrowed sharp enough to cut, and locked onto him. He held out one jar with an outstretched arm and summoned the courage to say something, anything.

"Peace offering," he said, immediately wishing he'd chosen better words.

She stared at it a long second, then took it. She didn't take a drink, but the simple fact that she accepted it was enough to let Butler know he could stay just a little while longer. Phoebe held the jar of sweet tea in her free hand while the rifle was still cradled in the crook of her other arm.

Brad's elbow found Juan's ribs with a sound like splitting oak. Juan answered with a knee that caught Brad in the thigh. Someone in the crowd whooped like this was the main event they'd paid extra for. Butler took a sip of his own tea. It tasted like East Texas summers and porch swings and a girl who used to laugh when he missed squirrels on purpose just to watch her shoot.

"I'm still using your techniques, you know," he said before she could cut him down or walk away or both. "Every single one. I remember all of 'em like it was yesterday. How you settled into the stock like the damn gun grew out of your own shoulder, how you told me time and time again that the trigger could only be squeezed at the top or bottom of your breath, how you floated those front sights in the only place a bullet, how you couldn't put your instinct into words about how a target had its own way of waiting for you. Every impossible shot I ever made online, every trophy, every sponsor check, every time the crowd lost their minds. That was all from what you taught me."

Her fingers tightened on the mason jar hard enough that the glass creaked. She didn't look away. "Don't forget how you stole my gun. Everythin' you've ever done wasn't what I taught you, it was what you took from me. And you're still doin' it to this day."

"I know," he didn't hold back.

"You built your whole damn life on it."

"I know," he repeated.

"You let them put your name on my dad's only heirloom meant to be mine, you built a legacy on the shoulders of my family. You knew what that rifle was, you knew who it once belonged to, and you did it anyway."

"I know."

"Do you know the irony behind what you're doing now, though? How you're using the same rifle Annie Oakley made her livin' with tourin' with ol' Buffalo Bill to win the *Texas Sure Shot*? If you had a lick of decency in ya, you wouldn't even show your face."

Juan broke loose and tackled Brad into the side of the train car and metal rang out loud enough to punctuate Phoebe's last sentence to Butler. She took a step closer, getting close enough to smell gun oil and pine. "I watched you up there," she said. "On the roof of that damned train. You shot like it was nothing, like you didn't even have to try. That's 'cause of me. You haven't had to try a goddam thing in life, not really, because you took it all from me and my family."

The words hit harder than any fist Juan was throwing ten feet away. Butler felt them land square in his chest and stay there, heavy as the Winchester itself. Juan had just slammed Brad against the side of the train car again—metal rang out like a cracked bell—and the crowd answered with a roar that rose and fell like a wave. Dust hung thick in the air, tasting of iron and sweat and old mistakes. Butler swallowed. The sweet tea in his hand had gone warm already.

"I did," he said this time, quieter now, like saying it louder might make it less true. "I know what I took. I know what I kept taking every time I pulled that trigger in front of a camera. I know the rifle never forgot whose hands it learned in, even when I pretended it was mine."

Phoebe's eyes didn't leave his. They were the same mix of honest naivety and twisted selfishness they'd been when they were ten and she'd dared him to hit a pine cone at a hundred yards. He'd missed so bad the bullet whined off into the creek.

Behind them, Brad flipped Juan over his hip and back into the concrete. Juan hit the ground hard, air dislodging out of him in a grunt you could hear over the shouting. Brad followed him down, knee in the small of Juan's back, twisting an arm until something popped and Juan howled. The crowd howled louder, masking his pain with a kind of interest that belonged to surrounding an octagon at a UFC fight.

"You coulda wrote a letter," she said. "Coulda drove down that dirt road you knew good and well we were hidin' on and knocked on the door. Coulda said sorry with your own mouth instead of lettin' a rifle do your talkin' all these damn years."

"I was scared," he admitted, and the words tasted like rust. "Scared you'd look at me exactly the way you're lookin' at me right now. Scared you'd be right to hate me. And deep down, I guess I was scared that if I gave the rifle back too soon, I'd never see you again."

Phoebe laughed once, short and bitter. "So you kept it. Built a whole empire on it. Let 'em carve your name in the history books like it was nothin' more than another trophy. And now you stand here handin' me sweet tea like that fixes anything."

"No, ma'am," he said. "It don't fix a damn thing."

Juan was on his feet again somehow, blood streaming from his nose and cheeks and into the collar of his torn shirt, but that didn't stop him from swinging wild. Brad caught the punch on his forearm, answered with a short, ugly jab to Juan's ribs that folded him in half. The crowd surged forward, hungry for more.

Phoebe took one more step. Close enough now that Butler could see the faint freckles across her nose that the sun had brought back out, the same ones she'd had when they were kids running barefoot through the pine thicket.

"I could see the look in your eyes when you shot my rifle today," she said, voice low. "I saw it plain as day. Felt it in my gut when that ball turned to red smoke. That wasn't you shootin', Butler. That was that damned rifle rememberin' whose blood it came from."

Butler couldn't speak. His throat closed up tight, and he struggled to find the air needed to respond. He just stared at her with endless hopes and dreams that were being dashed with every word he could find the courage to say. His gaze lingered, even while over her shoulder, the fight was coming to a violent end.

Range officers had finally waded in. It took four of them to haul Brad and Juan apart from one another, enduring stray punches and kicks and spats like they were entering a riot in the streets. Juan was still screaming, voice hoarse now, blood bubbling at his nostrils. Brad stood loose, breathing hard, blood on his teeth, but his eyes were already somewhere far away. The crowd started to thin, buzzing like flies after the show was over.

Phoebe looked down at the .22 rifle leaning into her arms and spoke without making eye contact. "You do still shoot like me," she said, almost soft. "Don't think I didn't notice."

"Every time," he answered.

"That's somethin', I guess."

Butler couldn't respond, he lifted the mason jar to his lips but stopped just long enough to lock eyes with Phoebe for a split second.

She was the first to break from him, using another sip of tea to distract her. Then, she simply lifted the Remington back into her arms and turned to walk off through the settling dust, boots crunching gravel, never as much as flickering her eyes at the men desperate to beat each other senseless all around her.

Butler watched her go until she disappeared into the crowd heading for the chuckwagon tents. The mason jar in his hand was empty now, tea long gone, ice melted to lukewarm water. He stood there in the heat and the smell of blood and diesel and mesquite smoke, listening to Juan's voice fade into hoarse curses as they dragged him toward the medic tent.

Hearst was still leaning against the train car, gold

Colt catching the sun, smiling that same dead smile like he'd just found a new toy. Lena was already narrating the whole thing to her phone, words flying fast as the punches had. Brad wiped his mouth, picked up his rifle case, and walked off without a word or a limp.

Butler stood alone in the gravel with nothing but the taste of tea and regret thick on his tongue, knowing one thing for damn sure. The rifle would have to go back to her one way or another, and until it was, he would still be a long, long way from being forgiven.

Chapter 14

The sun rose to welcome another day just like it always did, no different than the trillion times it had done before. It was slow, deliberate, and somehow, always both invited and despised at the same time.

For Phoebe, the sun shone its light down on the earth just like the lid of hell cracking open to hurl its remains onto anything decent and kind, yet unfortunate enough to be in its vicinity. She watched as white fire danced across the fairgrounds until every blade of grass looked sharp enough to draw blood, and the air itself turned thick as molasses left too long in the jar. By eight that morning, the heat had already settled into Phoebe's bones. It was humid and uncomfortable for most, but for her, it was heavy, familiar, and impossible to shake. It was the same kind of heat she'd spent most of her time out in when others had more than a single window unit for air conditioning in their home.

She stood at the edge of the next competition that had been laid out overnight. It was more than five hundred yards of pasture stretching out in front of her in either direction she faced. A cool breeze touched her cheeks as she gazed out over the horizon dotted with the silhouettes of what most sane folks would call people. They stood out hundreds of yards away, unmoving, staring right back at Phoebe with endless intensity.

Except they weren't people. They were targets. Phoebe didn't realize this until one by one, they started falling backward until they couldn't be seen anymore. Then, just a few seconds later, one by one again, they stood right back up and kept staring at her. The silhouettes were nothing more than wooden cutouts, popping up like bad memories in the back of your mind. It looked simple enough, until about a hundred more identical targets popped up sporadically throughout the pasture at different distances, with targets placed at different spots on the silhouette, and each one falling at different intervals, only to pop right back up again.

Today would be all about endurance, and the rules were both simple and cruel. From nine that morning until the last ray of sunlight touched the earth, every shooter would keep shooting. There were no breaks to piss or puke, and you couldn't miss a single target throughout the day. One miss equaled one disqualification, simple as that.

The *Texas Sure Shot* had turned the endurance competition into an all-day event. Advertisers were buying up real estate left and right, vendors were setting up the same booths that seemed to follow the shooters wherever they went—chuck wagons for barbecue, stands for sweet tea, a million booths for soaps and jewelry and trinkets, and that one fried pie place that couldn't keep enough inventory to last the day.

It was becoming something of a welcome world for Phoebe. The competition was more of a show than anything else, and they were the contestants. They were the ones people were rooting for or against, falling in love with or hating more and more by the second. They were the ones that demanded attention, that put their dreams and livelihoods on the line, that put even the governor of the state at their beck and call.

There were only five of them left now. Brad Kremer, Will Randy Hearst, Lena Mitchell, Butler, and her. Phoebe's .22 lay on the bench in front of her like an old dog too loyal to quit. Beside that beat-up old rifle was the one that she should've been using, the Winchester that Butler had refused to give up. He couldn't even linger around long enough to make eye contact after their conversation the day before, but that was to be expected. Butler was the kind of man to ask for forgiveness rather than permission. Through the years, that had come to shape him in ways he couldn't even see. Phoebe knew she was the first to refuse his apology, she could see it every time they made eye contact. He didn't know what to do with himself when sorry didn't work.

The next thirty minutes saw the crowd begin to form, first halfhearted and quiet, before a dull roar got louder and louder and louder. The shooters trickled in behind them. Brad limped in with a swollen, busted bottom lip and a shiner you could spot from a mile away. Lena walked right behind him, paying attention only to the phone held high above her head, streaming every waking second just like normal. Hearst followed close, staring at Phoebe like a coyote circling its prey for reasons she still didn't understand. By the time everything was set and ready to go, Butler had managed to sneak in without being seen.

He glanced at Phoebe before darting his eyes away and reaching for the Winchester like it was a cookie jar he'd already gotten in trouble for robbing one too many times. He lined up to the roar of a crowd that only knew who he presented himself as online. If they'd known who he really was, it would've been a different kind of roar that rose up into the air every time he lifted that rifle, but they didn't know. They cheered and hollered and begged for signatures because they just didn't know any better.

Phoebe knew, though. She grabbed her Remington, which surprised her every time it fired straight, and cradled it like it was the only thing she had on her side in life. The announcer's voice finally cut off the crowd and interrupted her worst thoughts. She sat there lined up with the rest of the shooters, still trying to come to terms with the whirlwind that had become her life as the announcer explained the rules.

"Settle in for a long day, folks." His voice came through the megaphone. "We've got thousands of targets, thousands more in ammunition, and nothin' but time to watch these shooters show their worth. So, grab some brisket and a sweet tea and kick your feet up."

The crowd came to life once again as the projector screen focused on each of the shooters like they were going on trial after the perp walk was completed. They were anxious in their own right, Phoebe was no different, all except for Hearst. Will Randy Hearst looked like he'd just gotten away with murder and couldn't wipe the smile off his face.

"Shooters, time to find your lane. That's gonna be

your office for the day. The sun sets at 8:38 p.m. tonight, so I hope you didn't have plans!"

The crowd laughed in response, but none of the shooters reacted. The announcer continued regardless.

"Here's what's gonna happen. We've got some sponsors who have kindly paid the wages of some folks who're gonna be runnin' ammo to you when you need a resupply. We've got more folks downrange ready to fix any target malfunctions that happen. And we've got even more who're keepin' tally of every single target you hit. All you gotta do is keep shootin'. If you miss once, that little red light at your booth is gonna flash, and the crowd is gonna let you know your time in the *Texas Sure Shot* has come to an end. You've got almost twelve hours to go, so I hope you had a big breakfast! When the clock strikes nine a.m., this little endurance competition is gonna kick off. But before that, we've got word that the governor would like to say something."

This time, Phoebe couldn't help but turn her attention to the projector behind them, just like everyone else at the fairgrounds. Governor Rourke's smiling face donned the screen for what this time was clearly a recorded message. He beamed and waved to a crowd he didn't even know was there before finally speaking up.

"Welcome, ladies and gents, to the third round of the *Texas Sure Shot* competition!" The preplanned pause for crowd eruption fell flat after the announcer had already covered the information, but the governor just kept going. "It's gonna be all day plinkin' out here, but miss one, and you are done! That's right, from sunup to sundown, y'all are gonna be shootin' one target after another. I wanna know which of you have what it takes not to just shoot one good time, but to do it over and over again. So, if you wanna go to the next round, the rules are simple. Don't miss. We're gonna call this round, *Shoot till you Drop*. Good luck, y'all!"

The horn blasted at nine sharp, punctuating the final farewell wishes from the governor like a dying bull dragged across gravel. The first silhouette snapped upright at two hundred and eleven yards, featuring a target across its chest that looked no larger than a silver dollar. Phoebe's .22 cracked before the echo died and the target dropped. Another popped at fifty yards, this time a head shot. The rhythm settled into her bones in a matter of minutes, and she felt right at home getting back to work.

As the crowd cheered the start of the celebration, it sounded like fireworks popping off all over the range. Each of the shooters did the same as Phoebe, focusing on the random targets popping up all over the field, squeezing the trigger at the last second to drag out the day as long as possible. They shot and shot and shot, and soon the crowd grew bored with the repetitive nature of the endurance competition. Their screams gave way to a few hollers as random as the targets that never ceased popping up in the field stretched out in front of the shooters.

Soon, everyone was settled into what the day would hold. It was a never-ending series of squeezing the trigger, reloading, then squeezing the trigger again. For the first few minutes, Phoebe was jealous of those who could bring in appropriate rifles. She glanced around at those who could hold more than one round, like Brad, who could fire off eight rounds even with a bolt-action. She thought of how easy it must've been to yank on that lever action of her old Winchester, then thought better of allowing her mind to drift toward Butler.

After the first hour, she was grateful for her little single-shot .22 rifle. The motion of ejecting a spent cartridge, jamming a tiny bullet into the barrel, and locking the bolt back into place before firing off a single round became cathartic. It was also something of an advantage for her. There was less time spent firing than anyone else in the competition. Even Hearst knew as much, he kept refusing to hide his sinister stares at her, and even flagged down one of the ammo runners at one point to file a formal complaint, as he called it rather loudly.

Phoebe just kept plinking away, watching for targets popping up that she could hit with her .22. She did her best to avoid those five-hundred-yard targets, knowing what little gunpowder was behind each bullet, she focused on the closest targets, only lobbing bullets when absolutely necessary.

By ten o'clock, she was already sweating through her shirt. The sun climbed higher in the blue skies overhead, turning the pasture into a skillet where shooters were tossed inside haphazardly to burn and wipe sweat from their eyes, all for an audience. Targets kept rising and falling, seemingly coming a little faster with each passing minute, drunk on the chaos that ensued between reloading and firing.

There was a two-hundred-yard torso shot, a fifty-yard left shoulder shot, a hundred-yard right leg shot, each one flashing a target that could easily be missed with the blink of an eye. Phoebe worked the bolt slick as lying, brass spinning into the dust to become nothing more than spent promises.

Across the lane, Brad Kremer stood as stoic as ever,

his .300 Win Mag bolt gun singing a deeper song in low, confident, thunderous roars. Every time he fired, the muzzle brake kicked a cone of dust that hung in the air a second longer than it had any right to. He never rushed nothing, blinked less. His prosthetic leg was planted solid in the dirt like God had nailed it there himself and then walked off without leaving instructions.

Farther down, Hearst left that forsaken gold Colt holstered at his hip, catching sunlight every time he leaned back for the long shots. For this round, he'd brought in a .30-30 lever-action with golden baroque scrolling and a custom octagon barrel. The lever-action had a forty-five-degree pull on it, making each reload a little bit faster than it should have been. If only he'd known that would be working against him in the endurance competition. He had a cigar clamped between teeth gone pale yellow, and smoke curled around his face like he was summoning something meaner than the Texas heat. Every time a target fell, he gave a little nod, as if the wood had personally offended him and was now apologizing properly.

Lena was the only one who was visibly struggling before the sun could reach high noon. She couldn't check her live stream from the phone resting on the bench in front of her, she couldn't check her messages still flooding into her inbox, she couldn't even put down the .308 rifle she'd used during the first round of the competition. The only thing she could do was keep her focus locked downrange and take it one shot at a time.

Phoebe could see the worry in her eyes, though. Endurance wasn't something Lena would excel at, she'd spent most of her life bouncing from one thing to the next without so much as a second thought.

Butler was last in line, and watching him hurt worse than the sun ever could, so Phoebe did her best to not stare for more than a few seconds. He had her rifle cradled like a baby he'd stolen in plain daylight. The Winchester spoke soft and certain, almost gentle, the way it always had when it was hers. Every bullet found its mark with lazy confidence. He never worked the action fast, he didn't have to. The rifle did half of the thinking for him, and the other half was muscle memory she'd burned into him when they were barefoot kids with pine sap on their hands. That rifle could go all day and never come close to missing a shot, the only thing Butler had to do was keep ammo cycling through it.

Phoebe hated him for how easy he made it look.

BY NOON, the chuckwagon had run out of brisket and started serving disappointment on a bun. Iced sweet tea became watered down until no one wanted anymore. Phoebe's tongue felt thick as felt wadding. Her shoulders burned like somebody had poured coal oil on them and struck a match. The .22 barrel was too hot to touch without gloves, and even through the leather, it felt like holding the cool end of a branding iron.

Targets soon started playing dirty. Two popped at once, one at five hundred, one at two-eighty. Then three came up at once, then four. The cadence went from steady heartbeat to machine-gun stutter. Phoebe's world narrowed to a simple series of motions, front sight, target, muzzle flash, bolt, front sight, target, muzzle flash, until she couldn't tell where her pulse ended and the rifle began.

A kid in a straw hat, no older than fifteen, ran the line with a cooler of water strapped to his chest. He hustled from one shooter to the next, doing his best not to interrupt the competition. Phoebe drank without taking the barrel off the bench, eyes never leaving the field. Water ran down her chin, soaked the collar of her shirt, mixed with sweat and gunpowder residue until she smelled like war and summer all at once.

Brad never slowed. Hearst never stopped grinning. Butler never missed. And Lena was becoming more frustrated by the minute.

One o'clock in the afternoon brought the first real test. The targets that popped up out in the pasture were suddenly holding out steel plates the size of pie pans, hung from chains clamped to what looked like outstretched hands on either side of the silhouette. It added yet another variable to consider when aiming, and every single one of the shooters groaned in unison at the revelation.

Phoebe watched the first plate dance, waited for the pause between gusts of an all-too-welcome breeze, and squeezed the trigger. Steel rang sweet and clear. She didn't smile, even if she wanted to, it was just energy she didn't have to give at the moment.

Hearst laughed out loud when his bullet kissed the steel plate no more than twenty-five yards away. He even had the bravado to raise a hand and urge the crowd to cheer on his less-than-impressive shot at such a close distance.

By the time it was Butler's turn, the plate just swung lazy in the heat shimmer. He exhaled half a breath—the exact way she'd taught him back in the woods—and the Winchester whispered. The plate jumped, and the crowd roared louder than it ever did for anyone else.

Phoebe felt it in her teeth and did her best to swallow the rage that boiled up inside her every time she thought about him holding that rifle.

Two o'clock came and went, minutes dragging by like hours until the clock struck three o'clock. The sun hammered down until the brass at her feet looked molten. Her counter read 623 hits and zero misses. She figured the other shooters were putting up similar numbers, considering none of them had been forcibly removed for missing a shot yet.

By four o'clock, the shadows finally started stretching long enough to be useful. Phoebe's shirt clung to her with every movement, drenched in sweat. Her vision blurred, narrowing down to the targets and nothing else. The .22 felt like it weighed forty pounds and was getting heavier by the second.

They saved the worst for last, because of course they did.

Every target that popped up was at least three hundred yards out. Gone were the easy fifty and hundred-yard shots, replaced by silhouettes popping up in faster intervals than ever before, with smaller targets than they'd ever seen. Silver dollars became quarters flashing in the dwindling sunlight, making every shot harder and harder. The wind slowly started to pick up too, providing a breeze to wick the sweat from their brow, but also pushing bullets just enough to turn a good shot into a graze and a graze into a miss that would end everything.

Phoebe's hands trembled now when she loaded the

single round, a fine shake she hid by gripping the stock tighter. The .22 wasn't made for this kind of distance, not with the drop and the wind and the tiny kill zones that danced like they knew how tired she was. She picked her shots carefully, letting the far ones go to the others if she could, snatching the closer ones before they vanished. The rhythm turned brutal, her fingers felt raw from the bolt, and her eyes burned from staring into the glare.

Brad's .300 kept thundering steady, each boom kicking dust high enough to choke on. He adjusted for wind like he'd fought it in deserts hotter than this, never wasting a round. Hearst's lever-action clicked and cracked faster than it should, his face redder now, sweat cutting trails through the cigar ash on his cheeks. He cursed under his breath every time the wind stole a fraction of an inch, but he hit anyway, stubborn as any veteran would surely be. Lena was cracking, and she couldn't hide it. Her .308 barked erratic, shoulders heaving like she was running a marathon with the rifle instead of shooting it. She kept glancing at her phone between shots, thumb twitching like it needed to scroll, to check likes, to escape this endless field of wood and heat. Phoebe saw it coming the way you see thunderclouds rolling in slow—the frustration building, the focus slipping, the shots getting rushed.

Butler, meanwhile, looked almost serene. The Winchester nestled against his shoulder, speaking soft truths with every pull of the trigger. He didn't fight the wind, he read it the way she'd taught him, holding half a breath, letting the rifle do what it had always done. The crowd chanted his name in waves now, drunk on his ease, blind to the brazen theft that made it all possible.

Five o'clock crept in and the light began to lie to each of the shooters. The sun hung lower, turning the pasture the kind of gold that you could only appreciate if you saw it in person. Phoebe's counter climbed past eight hundred, zero misses still glowing green. Her back ached like someone had taken a fence post to it, and her mouth tasted of brass and dust and gunpowder. The kid with the water came around again, but the bottles were warm now, tasting only of plastic.

The targets came in clusters—five, six, seven at once—popping up and falling back down again like some sadistic whack-a-mole. They had every right to be challenging, but with her dad's freedom on the line, every new round felt like a personal taunt on every fiber of her being. Phoebe's world was front sight and flash, the crack of her little .22 lost among the deeper roars. She felt the rifle's limits, felt the bullets drop more than they should at four hundred yards, held higher, prayed quieter than she had since her daddy went away.

Hearst barked something at an ammo runner, voice hoarse, demanding more cartridges like volume alone could make the day end sooner. Brad just reloaded methodically, face blank as carved oak. Lena's shots started skipping, her form breaking, elbows flaring, breath coming in angry huffs.

Six o'clock came like waiting for Christmas in July. The light turned orange, shadows long enough to trip over. Cicadas began their evening songs, screeching louder than the guns now, like they were mocking the whole show in a chorus that couldn't be ignored. Phoebe's arms shook when she lifted the .22, muscles screaming for mercy she couldn't give. She thought of her father, how he was locked away for something he didn't do, and she thought of the executive order waiting at the end of this nightmare, then squeezed again.

The crowd had thinned to the faithful and the foolish, voices hoarse from cheering, bellies full of fried pies and barbecue and too much alcohol. Butler was the name that most heard, but Phoebe slowly started to notice a different chant forming beneath the surface.

"Sure Shot! Sure Shot!"

The fans remembered what she did before the competition even began. They saw the look in her eyes, the sweat still pouring down her face, the struggle to even hold the blazing hot rifle, much less squeeze the trigger with any sense of accuracy. They cheered her past all of it.

SEVEN O'CLOCK BROUGHT YET another unspoken cruelty. Just about an hour and a half before the sun would finally give way to darkness, the silhouettes popping up changed completely. No longer were they fixed targets or swinging steel plates, they were leaning from side to side, swaying in the unpredictable breeze that sped up or slowed down the targets depending on where they revealed themselves.

Phoebe blinked sweat from her eyes, tasted blood where she'd bitten her lip too hard. Her counter read 892, but the numbers blurred, and the targets mocked her with their motion. The sun still clung to the horizon, bleeding slowly away behind the trees in the distance. Against every sensible notion she had inside her, she allowed herself a glance over at Butler to see how he was managing the final twist in the endurance competition.

Butler looked over at just the right moment, locking eyes with Phoebe with an unexpectedly worried demeanor, the Winchester heavy in his arms for the first time all day. His face was pale under the sunburn, eyes carrying a weight that hadn't been there at nine that morning. Phoebe held her gaze until he dropped his first. The light was fading fast, shadows swallowing the far targets, but the day wasn't done. Not yet. They both knew deep down that someone would fold before the light was gone, it was only a matter of time.

This morning, there were five shooters who remained to see the sunrise, but before it could set again in the west, there would only be four.

Chapter 15

At some point, when you've done all you can do, you have to just let go and say what everyone resigns themselves to that same old saying we've all heard a thousand times over—it is what it is.

Butler felt it in his shoulders first, then his lower back, that deep burn that said twelve hours was too much, but the Winchester cradled against his cheek didn't give a damn about his aches. It never did. It just waited patiently for him to line up the next shot and let it do what it did best. Never miss.

The targets were meaner now in the dying light, swaying drunk on their mechanisms like they knew the shooters were running on fumes. Three hundred yards minimum, some pushing five, kill zones shrunk to quarters that flashed and vanished quicker than a lawyer's promise. Every trigger finger still firing off rounds was worn smooth out. A single ounce too much pressure one way or another could end any of their dreams before they ever began. Somewhere, the governor was waiting for exactly that to happen.

Brad was still thundering away down the line, his .300 Win Mag barking slow and steady as always, each shot deliberate as the last. Hearst's lever-action clicked and cracked like it was arguing with him, his face slick with sweat that cut pale trails through the grime and cigar ash. He cursed low every time the wind stole an inch, voice raw as butcher paper.

Lena was coming apart at the seams, though. Butler could hear it in the erratic rhythm of her .308, it was like she was fighting the rifle instead of shooting it. Her shoulders heaved between shots, phone on the bench forgotten now but still glowing with notifications she couldn't check. She'd been flashy all day, narrating to nobody in particular when the crowd was thick, but the crowd had thinned to diehards and drunks, and endurance didn't care about followers or filters. It only cared about pure, unfiltered grit.

And Phoebe. God, Phoebe.

Butler didn't want to look, but his eyes kept dragging themselves back to her lane like a tongue to a sore tooth. She was a sight to be seen, that much was for sure. Her hair plastered dark with sweat, shirt clinging like wet paper, hands working that little .22 with the grim determination of a woman building her own coffin nail by nail. She was picking her shots carefully, letting the far ones go when she could, snatching the ones that popped closer like they were the last scraps of food in a hard winter. Something he knew she was unfortunately used to.

Her counter was climbing. Slower than his, slower than Brad's, slower than Hearst's, but climbing steady. The board showed her at 878 when he dared a glance, zero misses glowing green, like it was mocking the rest of them for having easier tools.

The crowd, or at least what was left of it, had started something ugly and beautiful at the same time. It began as a murmur, a few voices near the chuckwagon tents where the fried pie man had long since packed up and gone home. Then it spread, hoarse and drunk and earnest, rolling across the pasture like distant thunder.

"Sure Shot! Sure Shot! Sure Shot!"

They weren't cheering for him, not anymore.

Butler felt it land in his gut like an uppercut he couldn't dodge. They were chanting for her, for the girl with the beat-up .22 who was outshooting people with rifles that cost more than she'd ever seen in her lifetime, for the girl who'd gunned down the would-be murderer of the governor of the state of Texas, for the girl who was bleeding sweat and willpower for one chance to make things right with her wrongfully imprisoned father, most importantly, for the girl whose rifle he was holding.

The Winchester felt heavier suddenly. Butler's palms were slick inside his gloves, not just from heat but from something colder. Guilt had a unique taste, like that metallic twinge you get from biting the inside of your cheek too hard and drawing blood. He tasted that guilt now with every breath, but that was nothing new. He should've given it back. He knew that. He should have done what was right years ago. Any time before he lined up with it cradled like it was his birthright. He could've walked over before the horn, set it on her bench with a quiet "I'm sorry" that might've meant something. She would've taken it. Might've even looked at him without that knife-edge hate in her eyes.

That's not what he did, though. His sponsors were

watching just like always, the cameras were rolling, the people were hanging onto every bullet that blasted out of the end of his rifle. His whole damn life, the trophy room, those impossible shots, the commercials where he grinned like a man who'd earned every bit of it—was built on this rifle and the lie that it was his skill alone. He couldn't give it back now, or at least that's what he told himself so he could sleep at night. The second he gave away the truth about his rifle, he'd watch the empire he worked so hard for crumble into the dust.

He thought about what it might feel like to finally do the right thing, then he squeezed the trigger instead. The Winchester whispered its soft truth yet again, and another target dropped clean at four hundred yards away. The rifle didn't care about his guilt, it never did. He never had to reason his ways with it, he only had to squeeze the trigger again and again and again.

As he carried on without missing a beat, he forgot there were shooters still in the competition that weren't himself and Phoebe. Brad looked like he couldn't be bothered, and Hearst clearly had it out for Phoebe the way he kept mocking every single thing she did. Butler wasn't sure if the crowd had gotten to him or if he'd just plain old gone crazy. What he should have noticed, however, was Lena.

She wasn't just struggling, she was breaking down.

It was eight o'clock. They only had thirty-eight more minutes to keep firing. Between them all, they'd shot thousands of targets without a single miss, something that must've been both boring and exhilarating to watch as an innocent bystander. The day was beginning to take its toll, though, especially for Lena.

It wasn't dramatic at first. Just a small plate they had seen dozens of times before in the day that popped up at the four hundred twenty-yard marker. It leaned from side to side just like the rest, but Lena must've calculated wrong. Her bullet clipped the edge of the silhouette, sending wooden shards splintering in the air, but the steel plate never rang. It hung lifelessly, hundreds of yards away, without making a sound until the red light flashed bright as fresh blood on her booth. The buzzer wailed long and ugly, cutting through the cicadas and the chants and the dying gunfire.

Lena froze. She stared at the target like she was waiting for the bullet to come back around and strike the steel. Then, she slammed the .308 down hard enough to rattle the bench, kicked the legs out from under it, and let loose a string of curses that would've made a sailor blush. Her phone was in her hand before the range officers even reached her, thumb flying across the screen as she stormed off the line, live-streaming her meltdown to whatever followers were still awake.

The crowd gave her a halfhearted boo, more tired than mean. A few clapped like it was part of the show. Most just turned back to the four shooters still standing, the chant swelling louder now that the field had narrowed.

"Sure Shot! Sure Shot! Sure Shot!"

Butler felt it in his teeth. In his bones. In the stock of the rifle pressed against his cheek like a brand.

Phoebe didn't acknowledge any of it. She didn't wave. She didn't smile. She just kept working that .22 with the single-minded focus of a woman who'd learned long ago that the world didn't give you anything—you just had to take it. Her hands shook now when she loaded each small round into the firing chamber, but she pushed ahead anyway.

Her counter hit 900. Then 905. Closing the gap one painful round at a time. Butler's was at 923. Brad's 921. Hearst 919. The board glowed green across the line, no red except Lena's frozen at 889, a monument to impatience.

The sun was finally sinking below the horizon proper now, bleeding orange and red across the sky as darkness crept in all around them. Light was tricky, long shadows lying across the field, making distances hard to read, kill zones disappearing into glare one second and flashing bright the next. Wind died to nothing, then gusted hard enough to shove a man sideways.

Butler's arms had long become as heavy as lead. His eyes burned from staring down the sights all day. His shirt was soaked through, boots full of sweat and ejected brass that once burned, but had now cooled. The Winchester didn't care about any of it. The gun kept firing, and the bullets kept hitting their target. All Butler had to do was go through the motions and the next round would be a given.

For just a split second, he thought about missing on purpose, about letting the red light flash and the crowd turn and walk away knowing the truth, about letting the rifle go home. The sponsors would come, though. Eventually, the toll must be paid. He'd already cashed in as much as he could, there were phone calls that had to be answered, contracts that had to be completed. Sure, his life had been built on impossible shots, but there were also the impossible lies he couldn't avoid.

He lined up another swaying target at five hundred yards, wind holding steady for once, and squeezed.

Another target fell, and by the grace of something bigger than him, it would be his last shot.

The horn finally sounded at 8:38 p.m. on the dot, long and mournful. The targets stopped popping. The mechanisms whirred to silence. The field went still except for the cicadas and the dying breeze.

When the smoke cleared, there were four shooters remaining. Butler topped the scoreboard, for what little it was worth, with 942 targets hit. Brad Kremer came in second with 940, followed by Will Randy Hearst at 938 and Phoebe Anne just shy of Hearst at 937. There were four green lights, and one flashing bright red, but Lena was already gone.

The crowd had gone from what seemed like thousands that morning to maybe a hundred people. They gave out a ragged cheer that died quickly. They were too tired for much else, too drunk, too sunburned. They started shuffling toward the parking fields, boots dragging in the dust, leaving behind a pasture littered with brass that glinted like fool's gold in the last light.

Butler set the Winchester down gently on the bench, hands cramping into claws when he finally let go. His legs felt like they'd been poured in concrete and left to set. Brad was already packing his gear methodically, face blank as ever, prosthetic leg planted solid. Hearst lit another cigar with shaking hands, gold Colt back on his hip, eyes narrowed across the lanes at Phoebe like he was already planning tomorrow's dirty tricks.

Phoebe just stood there a second, staring at the field like she couldn't believe it was over. Then she laid the .22 down and rolled her shoulders slowly. She didn't look triumphant, but didn't look defeated either. She just looked done in, the way a prizefighter looks after fifteen rounds. She was still standing, but only just.

The chant had died with the horn. "Sure Shot" faded into coughs and truck doors slamming and engines turning over in the distance. Silence settled heavy as the heat had been all day.

Butler wanted to say something. He wanted to walk over with the Winchester case and set it at her feet and walk away before she could spit in his face. He wanted to tell her she'd earned it twice over today, that he was sorry in a way that might mean something. But the weight was too much, and his lie was too big. Those forsaken cameras were still rolling somewhere, he could still hear the faint trace of drones buzzing overhead like vultures waiting for the carcass to cool.

He grabbed the case instead, slung it over his shoulder, and turned toward the competitor tents before she could look his way. His boots crunched brass with every step, shoving empty brass casing deeper into the soil. The Winchester bounced against him, its weight on his back more than it had ever been in his hands.

Phoebe never called out to him, no matter how much he wanted her to. Everything inside him screamed and raged to come face to face with her again and right his wrongs, but every chance he got, he pissed away. From what he could tell, she never even looked up to watch him leave. She'd given up on him.

He knew tomorrow would bring new cruelties and new challenges, but also more heartbreak. He knew he didn't have the spine to bow out of the competition. He thought about the empty promise he'd given Phoebe, about how he could set it all right if he could just win that executive order from the governor. Then, he thought about how it would all play out, and he knew all he'd done was lie again. The sponsors and shareholders who signed his check wouldn't allow any such thing. He'd only take Phoebe's future with his own win, the same way he stole her past, but as he walked away, he settled into the same mindset that carried him from one day to the next. Those were all tomorrow's problems.

Tonight, there was only silence, and the taste of regret he couldn't get rid of.

Chapter 16

Sometimes the only thing left to do is wallow in loneliness.

Life always has a way of coming at you when you least expect it, that much everyone has to learn one way or another. What do you do when it never stops, though? You learn to cope with as much of it as best you can, but ultimately, after taking hit after hit, you find solace in the simplicity of being lonesome. When family is long gone and friends never even bothered to show up, when the world has it out for you, there is comfort to be found in the only thing you have left—yourself.

Such a downtrodden place was exactly where Phoebe found herself after the endurance round of the *Texas Sure Shot Competition.* The fairgrounds had emptied, the other shooters had gone home or to their hotel, and she was left alone to her own vices, which tonight consisted of leftover brisket that was colder than the watered-down sweet tea she had. Even so, she was thankful for the couple of vendors who were kind enough to set aside something for her. She ate and drank in silence, allowing the realization that she was one step closer to freeing her dad to settle in.

She sat on an overturned crate behind the chuck-wagon tents, the kind of spot nobody claimed because it smelled faintly of grease and old smoke and trash from a day's worth of work. The night air had finally cooled enough to raise goose bumps on her arms, but it felt good, like the first honest thing the day had offered her. Crickets sawed away in the dark, and somewhere a generator coughed itself to sleep. The big lights were off now, just a few security floods casting long yellow pools across the dirt, flickering only against the spent brass scattered around the mud.

Phoebe chewed slowly, tasting more salt and fatigue than hickory-smoked meat. Her hands still trembled when she lifted the mason jar of tea, fine shakes she couldn't quite hide from herself anymore. Nearly twelve hours of squeezing that single-shot .22 had left her fingers raw inside the gloves, palms blistered where the bolt handle had kissed them again and again. She set the jar down and allowed her thoughts to drift wherever they wanted. She was too exhausted for anything close to discipline.

One round closer. The words circled her mind like a moth around a dying bulb. There were only four shooters left of the original seven who kicked it off. Lena's red light still burned behind her eyes every time she blinked. She was just scraping by, holding onto every shot like her life depended on it. Each bullet became the only thing that separated her from going home empty-handed and watching her dad rot another year, another ten, another lifetime. Every time a bullet struck its intended target, she thought of just how little Butler had to do. She was too tired to stay mad for now, that'd have to wait until tomorrow.

Then, her thoughts turned to the crowd. They'd labeled her *Sure Shot* like the competition was stealing her own moniker. They'd chanted it until the horn blew, until the light died, until the last drunk stumbled to his truck. They'd given her the title like she'd already won the competition. When she found herself wondering what they'd call her if she failed now, she pushed the worries back down and tried to think of something, anything else.

She wiped her mouth with the back of her hand and stared out at the empty pasture. The silhouettes were gone now, hauled away or folded flat, but she could still see them in the dark—hundreds of them popping up, staring at her with blank wooden faces, waiting for her to prove she was still worth something. They were nothing more than ghosts, but she couldn't get them out of her head.

Her shoulders ached, and so did her arms. It was the kind of hurt that settled deep into the bone and promised to stay a while. She rolled them slow, felt the pop and grind of joints that had forgotten what rest felt like. Then, she leaned her head back against the tent pole, allowing her eyes to drift shut for just a second. The faces came without warning in her mind, her mom's tired smile when the garden didn't yield enough, her dad's hands showing her how to settle into the stock like the rifle was an extension of her own body. Soon after the faces came to her, so did the trauma. The day the sheriff took her dad away in cuffs. The way Butler had stood there holding the Winchester like it was already his, eyes wide and sorry, but not sorry enough to ever give it back. She opened her eyes before the sting behind them turned into something she couldn't swallow.

The fairgrounds were quiet in a way big cities never were. No traffic hum and screeching brakes, no neighbors arguing through thin walls, no sirens, no arguments unfolding in the middle of the street, just the low rustle of wind through mesquite and the occasional coyote yipping far off in the distance. Phoebe liked it. She liked the way the dark pressed in close, hiding the banners and the booths and the scoreboard that still glowed faintly in her mind.

She finished the brisket before it could get any colder, licked grease and barbecue sauce from her fingers, and stood up straight even though her body hated her for it. Her knees popped loud in the stillness. The .22 was back in its scabbard, slung over her shoulder. She thought about heading to the cot set aside by the old man running the official chuck wagon, but her feet carried her in another direction instead. She moved quietly past the empty lot that was filled with vendors only hours ago, past the darkened stages where an acoustic band played covers to sunburned crowds, out toward the edge of the grounds where the lights didn't reach.

The rifle range was a black void now, stretching out forever, lost in the shadows of night. Phoebe walked through it anyway, boots crunching soft, until she stood where her lane had been. She could almost feel the bench under her elbows, the heat of the barrel, the endless rhythm that had carved itself into her muscles. It was like she'd finished a road trip that took all day and could still feel herself driving down the road even when sitting still. There was a small part of her that didn't know how to quit, that didn't want to.

She set the .22 down gentle in the dirt and sat beside it, knees drawn up, arms wrapped around them. The ground was still warm from the day's punishment, radiating up through her jeans like a promise that tomorrow would try to kill her all over again. Doubt crept in, quiet as a snake through dry grass at first, then blaring in her skull until it was the only thing she could think about.

If only she had her old Winchester. None of this would've ever worried her. She would never have to wonder if she was going to hit her next target or make it to the next day in the hopes of seeing her dad again at the end of it all. She would never have to pray for her next meal before she knew where it would be coming from. She would never have to hate Butler again.

There was an ache deep down inside her gut to forgive Butler for what he'd done. Such feelings burned away before they ever had a chance to take hold. The fury she held inside her for that man refusing to fulfill a promise he made her was burning the same way it did when she had to hand that rifle over. She might've been better off keeping it and letting the police haul it away with her dad, maybe then she could've gotten it back. There was no use reminiscing on things that couldn't be changed. If she thought like that for too long, she'd start regretting her entire life. Everything from how she treated her mom after they were left alone to how she treated herself. Thinking like that was nothing more than a waste of time, she was at least smart enough to know that.

She kneeled down on one knee and picked up a piece of brass, turned it over in her fingers while she tried to force down every terrible feeling threatening to boil over inside of her. The brass casing was cool now, just a hollow shell, something she felt immediately connected with. She flicked it into the dark and listened to it ping off something metal far away, just like the thoughts she was getting rid of.

She hadn't cried since the day they took her dad. Not once, or at least not really. There were plenty of tears, but not the kind of cry that you regret in the middle of. The kind of cry that leaves you begging for oxygen, letting out nothing but wails and a red face, and nothing left to show for it. All she was left with after that day was hatred, and she was more than willing to unleash it on anyone who dared cross her. The truck full of drunks came for rent money, the trucker who turned mean, the boy who looked her in the eye and made a promise, and the man who failed to keep it. Tonight was no different, the burn was there behind her eyes still, hot and stubborn as ever. But she was also tired, tired all the way past her bones and deep down into her soul.

A footstep crunched behind her, soft and deliberate. Phoebe didn't turn around. She didn't care enough to see who it was.

"Evenin', miss."

The voice was nothing but gravel and smoke, thick with years mixed with something that might've been whiskey once upon a time that ripened it to nothing but a raspy whisper. Phoebe finally looked over her shoulder to see a man she didn't recognize.

He was ancient, there was no other way to describe him. He leaned up against a fence post like he'd grown there, a long white beard flowing down to his chest, hat battered enough to have its own history, eyes sharp and black under the brim that hung as low as his beard. A long leather jacket hung off shoulders that had probably been broad once, giving him an odd presence. No one in their right mind would wear such a heavy jacket in this heat and humidity. The old man was either senile or stupid, or a combination of the two. It was the first thing that told Phoebe she shouldn't listen to a single word he said.

Instead, she tensed up, allowing her hand to drift toward the .22. Her eyes darted back and forth until she locked onto the old man and sent daggers through him.

He raised both palms high into the air, slow and empty. "Ain't here to bother you none," he said without any sense of alarm in his voice. "Just saw a girl sittin' alone with a rifle and a face full of somethin' I know all too well myself. Figured she might could use company, or at least somebody to tell her she ain't the first to start feelin' like the world's done chewed her up and spit her out."

Phoebe relaxed a fraction. "I'm fine."

The old man chuckled, low and dry. "That's what they all say. Till they ain't. Sometimes they keep sayin' it, too. They keep lyin' to themselves like that feelin' will go away all on their own."

He eased himself down onto the ground a respectful distance away, joints popping like gunfire in the quiet. Up close, she could see the lines etched deep around his eyes, the kind you earn from squinting down rifle barrels in sun and dust for decades. His hands bore calluses thick as saddle leather, and there was a faint scar running across his knuckles shaped like an old powder burn. It wasn't whiskey that she heard in his voice, it was plain old beer, and it was still all over his breath. The man was a drunk.

They sat in silence for a while, just the crickets and the gentle breeze, interrupted by an occasional smoker's cough, blurted out by the old man. Phoebe waited for him to speak again, to ask for an autograph or tell her how pretty she shot or some other nonsense people had been throwing at her all week. He didn't do any of that, though. He just stared out at the dark field like he could see those same ghosts standing where the targets had been. When he did finally speak, his voice carried across the breeze so soft that Phoebe felt like the words may disappear before she could ever hear them.

"That Winchester your man's shootin' has a story, don't it?"

Phoebe's head snapped around. "He ain't my man."

The old man nodded slow, like that was answer enough. "Fair enough. You wanna tell me the story?"

She hesitated. "Not particularly," she said before regretting it instantly. Something about the night, about the emptiness, about the way his eyes didn't pry but waited patient as stone made her keep talking. "It belonged to my dad before it was mine. Before that…" She shrugged. "It sounds stupid, but my dad always said that gun was nothin' short of a legend, he said it went back further than the railway we lived next to. Most people don't even know who Buffalo Bill was these days, much less the people who performed for him."

The old man whistled low. "Little Annie Sure Shot. You don't got to say anythin' else. I had a feelin' I knew what was goin' on out there today, just couldn't prove it until now. If only that gun could talk."

Phoebe felt her throat tighten. "Just a story, like you said."

"Maybe, maybe not." He turned his head to look at her fully for the first time. His eyes were pale blue, faded but sharp, his mouth twitched for just a second before his gaze became still and undying. "I knew a man once, he was a shooter not unlike yourself, back when it was all tents and trains, back when folks paid a nickel to see miracles. He watched Annie Oakley herself put holes in playin' cards at fifty paces back. Said she shot a sweet as a hymn on Sunday morning after a night out drinkin'. He watched her shoot dimes outta the air, said she could make a grown man believe in magic. When she passed away, we all figured it was just the end of an era. Time has a way of leavin' people like that in the past. But you see, those weren't just some old stories, those were legends."

Phoebe stared at him. The night felt suddenly thinner, like the stars were leaning in to listen.

"One day, I heard about a boy out in East Texas doin' things that no man oughta be able to do," the old man continued. "That's when I knew."

Phoebe's mouth went dry. "Knew what?"

"It was back," he said. "Annie Oakley's rifle was back to stun the world. When you live as long as I have, you learn a few things. You learn that legends are just about the only thing time can't kill."

"I don't need that gun to win." She turned to face him, starting an argument with the man even when she wasn't certain if it should've been against herself. "I made it this far without it, I can win whether I'm shootin' that old rifle or not."

"Didn't say you couldn't," he answered.

"Then what are you sayin'?"

"I'm sayin' it's real. That man might be good with the gun that isn't his. But in the right hands it's somethin' else entirely. It's supposed to be yours, and don't think for a second that that fine piece of metal and wood filled with gunpowder doesn't know any better. It remembers."

"You must be drunker than I thought, old man," she said. "Who are you, anyways?"

"I'm a drunk old man," he answered with a smirk. "Just like you said."

Phoebe looked at him with all the uncertainty she could muster. He just stared right back, without a care in the world. She wondered for a second if he was even real or if she'd lost her mind entirely. Everything in her world was solely focused on the competition, on the opportunity it could provide her, anything that didn't have to do with that seemed not just irrelevant, but unreal. As her thoughts drifted to those of a more insane nature, the old man shattered every expectation she formed in a single sentence.

"What are you gonna do to change the world when it's yours again?"

"The hell does that mean?"

"You know what it means, Phoebe," he answered.

He immediately sparked her curiosity as to whether or not she told him her name, but then she remembered that probably the whole state of Texas knew her name at this point.

"It means that gun belonged to a legend, and she knew what to do with it. She took it around the world, changing how people thought about the west, about women, and what was really possible. That's why we still know her name. Annie Oakley made that gun what it is today, so the only question you've gotta answer is, what would you do with it?"

"In case you're blind on top of bein' drunk, I don't actually have the gun. That man—"

"Butler, yes, I know," he cut her off. "We've seen what he's done with it. He chased fortune and fame, just like anyone else would. But he'll learn soon enough where that gets him."

"How did you know—"

"The gun knows where it belongs, and before too long, it'll be in your hands. You might wanna think about what happens next, that's all I'm sayin'. Just remember, a gun ain't nothin' more than a tool, and a tool ain't no use to someone who don't know how to work."

With the final words having left his lips, he spat out a wad of something too nasty to look at and did his best to stand upright. His knees and hips cracked, and he groaned the whole way up, but he never lost eye contact with Phoebe.

She watched him brush off his pants and do something with his leg to make sure he could still walk right. Tobacco and leather and the kind of musk that comes from not showering for days and days hit her like a wave and turned her nose upright, forcing her to break the stare he'd initiated. When she looked back for him, he was already gone. There were no footsteps or ached grunts as he left the fairgrounds, he'd simply disappeared as quick as he'd shown up.

She shook off the chill creeping up her spine and looked up at the stars, hard and bright and endless. It was hard enough to think about the next round in the competition, much less what comes after it's all said and done, but maybe that wouldn't be true for long. She was closer now than ever before to what she wanted most. The doubt was still there, swirling in her guts and threatening to spill out of her every time she opened her mouth, but there was something else there too.

For the first time in what felt like forever, something warmer flickered inside her, something that felt like hope, or at the very least, the promise of a reckoning long overdue.

Chapter 17

Some days, you just wake up on the wrong side of the bed. You twist your ankle climbing out, you forget to brush your teeth and put on deodorant, and you leave your wallet in yesterday's pants. As the saying goes, sometimes, it doesn't even pay to get out of bed.

Phoebe's mood wasn't sour when she opened her eyes, in fact, it was quite the opposite, but the day had nothing good in store for her. It had quickly become a game to find out what would go wrong next. It started with something small, yet remarkably annoying. She'd lost one of her only socks, which left her with just one for the day. It was trivial, but it was just the start. Her breakfast came in colder than the dinner she had the night before. She slammed her finger in the door to the back of the chuckwagon when she finished eating. Then, to top it all off, she tripped over someone else's backpack that shouldn't have been in the middle of the only aisle to walk on.

By the time she'd picked herself up off the ground, shook the dirt loose from her palms and elbows, and gathered what little belongings she had, the warm positivity she'd woken up with had soured into bitter curses beneath her breath.

It was the first time they didn't have to travel for the next round of the *Texas Sure Shot* competition, and that was at least one thing to be grateful for. The last few days had become a whirlwind that was difficult to keep up with. Today, the fourth round of competition would be held in the same field as yesterday's endurance round, and there was something about the familiarity of the land that gave Phoebe a boost in her confidence. Whether or not it was just a placebo effect would have to be found out, but for now, she could at least take comfort in the fact that she wouldn't find herself in yet another unfamiliar environment.

The fairgrounds had once again traveled back in time to the Wild West, where stringed bands played along to boots stomping in the mud, men drinking long before the sun struck noon, and the smell of smoked meat and manure found its way everywhere you went. While Phoebe was trying to sleep, it seemed the whole state chipped in to set up another rodeo arena, horseback trail riding experience, target practice shooting range, a mock saloon and jailhouse for photographs, and a million vendor booths hawking items nobody needed.

The appeal had long worn off for Phoebe, and while the fans and tourists found plenty to entertain themselves with, she had nothing but her own racing thoughts to keep her occupied. She thought about what that old man told her last night, about the look on Butler's face knowing he was kicking her while she was down, and about how a single missed shot could send her packing just like it did to Lena.

The crowd was easily double the size of the day before, and there were still plenty of folks crammed shoulder to shoulder along the fences, trying their damndest to get in to watch the next round. Word had obviously spread overnight, and Phoebe had already started to hear whispers that Governor Rourke was going to be in attendance. He'd be rolling in with his motorcade of black SUVs and polished boots soon enough, his smile wide and white for the cameras.

People had driven in from every corner of the state, trucks parked clear out to the horizon, tailgates down, coolers open, kids running wild with foam cowboy hats and plastic six-shooters. The air hummed with excited chatter, the twang of banjos warming up, the sizzle of brisket on grills that never seemed to run out. Drones buzzed overhead like a swarm of mechanical locusts, and every phone in the place was held high, ready to capture whatever miracle or disaster came next.

Phoebe stood at the competitor gate, even though it was still morning, the sun had already started beating down hot enough to make yesterday's endurance feel like a warm-up. The main arena had been transformed with fresh rope barriers, hay bales stacked for cover, and a long shooting line with tables loaded with boxes of ammo. The stages were laid out clear as day on the big screens overhead. A double-barrel shotgun to split two clays launched high and crossing fast, a revolver to fan six playing cards tossed skyward, and the finale, a wretched act of shooting a glass ball into the air before exploding it mid-flight with the rifle before it could touch the ground. It was a classic twist on the modern three-gun competition, and Phoebe was woefully unprepared for just about all of it.

She wasn't the only one who would be hobbled, though. For the first time in the whole competition, Butler couldn't lean on her Winchester. He would have to shoot guns that didn't know his name, that could actually miss a shot. She might not have fancy tools, but she had hands that remembered, and she'd spent her whole life up close and personal with firearms that were all too eager to miss every shot. Butler, on the other hand, had used her family's gun as a crutch. All those bad habits were about to make themselves known for the world to see. That single thought put a spark in her chest hotter than the sun on the back of her neck.

She didn't own a proper shotgun, much less a wheel gun that could take on the challenge. Luckily, for this competition, a bunch of local firearm dealers had gotten together to offer a stack of loaners that each shooter could use. They were mostly old side-by-sides with barrels worn thin from honest work, Colt clones that felt heavy but hadn't actually been put to the test, and beat-up hunting rifles that had seen better days.

Phoebe spent the next couple of hours wandering through shops she couldn't afford to support, drooling over food she couldn't afford to eat, and imagining herself dressed in clothes she couldn't afford to wear. She found herself dreaming of living a normal life like the thousands of people scurrying back and forth, rushing to spend every penny they could on things they didn't actually need. Her meager life of necessity had drilled certain expectations of the real world into her head, but what she was experiencing in the brief moments of clarity between bouts, where her entire future was on the line, was nothing like what she thought it would be.

BEFORE SHE KNEW ANY BETTER, the competition that was once hours away was only minutes away, and she was no more prepared than when she tried to crawl out of her bed earlier that morning. She was standing in line with the other shooters when she noticed the competition wasn't nearly as friendly as it was only days ago. Brad and Butler were whispering back and forth about nothing important, and Hearst couldn't take his eyes off of her. He had nothing short of murderous intent filling him to the brim, and it was all directed right at Phoebe for reasons she didn't entirely understand. The only thing she did know was that she hated him every bit as much as he hated her.

They each walked up to the stack of loaner firearms and one by one, made their selection. It wasn't until she was up close to the guns that she realized they were attempting to be period-specific. They were antiques, not guaranteed to even fire correctly, but it was all they had access to. Phoebe begrudgingly picked a battered Parker side by side that balanced sweet despite the dents, and a Single Action Army with grips worn smooth by generations of thumbs. The .22 was still hers, though—scratched stock, barrel hot from the memory of yesterday, the only piece of this circus that belonged to her outright.

The shooting order came up on the screen behind them as they were loading all three of the firearms. Hearst first, Brad second, Butler third, and Phoebe coming in last. She groaned when she finally saw the order, knowing there was nothing she could do about it.

Hearst swaggered to the front of the line like he

owned all of their souls already, gold Colt flashing on his hip, an engraved Ithaca shotgun cradled in the nook of his arm, and his 6.5 Creedmoor he'd used back in the first round where he split a bullet in half on the edge of a blade. He could shoot just fine, and he knew it better than anyone else, but he was alone in his belief that it warranted such pretentious, cocky behavior.

The crowd gave him a roar that was half love and half hate. It was the kind of noise that was loud enough to mask the boos to most, but not to Hearst. He basked in it anyway, taking his time as he broke the Ithaca open, slid in two shells fat as his ego, and snapped it shut with a flourish.

There was no announcer today hollering through a megaphone. The screens panned from one shooter to the next, shot by a dozen buzzing drones that swarmed overhead like gnats over a hot meal. After the four familiar faces flashed across the screen, there was finally one that started talking. It was Governor Rourke.

He was among the crowd with all the screaming fans and smiling families, shaking hands and hugging anyone who'd let him when the camera finally focused in on him. When he realized what was happening, he feigned surprise and then smiled. It stretched across his face wider and wider before any words came out.

"Well, look at what we have here!" he screamed as the crowd went wild. "We are down to the final four of the first-ever *Texas Sure Shot* competition, and boy, has it been a sight for sore eyes. If you thought the days of gunslinging justice were long behind us, just take a look at those four standin' down there. They could shoot off another man's trigger finger from a mile away without even lookin', I'd bet every dollar I had on it!"

He looked around with that stupid smile plastered on his face and lifted his hands to urge the crowd on a little more. Phoebe watched on the screen and did her best not to roll her eyes at the only man who had the power to get her dad out of prison.

"Welcome to the fourth round, ladies and gents, this is the one that'll separate the boys from the men" —his voice trailed off for a moment—"and women, mind you." His hand gestured to Phoebe, and the crowd went wild with that all too familiar chant.

"Sure Shot! Sure Shot! Sure Shot!"

"Easy, easy," the governor coaxed, growing a bit uncomfortable the moment all the attention turned away from himself. "If yesterday was all about endurance, then today is nothin' but skill. One gun just ain't gonna cut it anymore. We're gonna find out real soon who has what it takes to be at that final round where the winner is chosen. One shotgun blast for two clay pigeons, six old-fashioned playin' cards fanned with a slap of the hammer, and a trick shot the world hasn't seen in generations—bouncin' a glass ball into the air and blowin' it to smithereens before it can fall. Shooters, welcome to the *Three Gun Split*!"

The crowd cheered, fireworks popped, and drones rose up into the air in a perfect circle, capturing those grandiose few seconds for the world to see. Governor Rourke had his hands lifted high into the air when the screen cut away from his face to show the first shooter taking his place at the lane.

The clays launched in tandem with the final burst of fireworks, and two orange streaks crossed high and fast against the blue sky that remained. The crowd's cheers went from screaming and hollering to gasps as Hearst swung his shotgun in a fluid circular motion, tracking each of the targets hurling through the air. Just before it was too late, the targets crossed, and Hearst squeezed the trigger.

A loud *boom* rang out across the field, echoing through the bleachers packed with fans, the vendor booths waiting on stragglers passing through willing to make a spur-of-the-moment purchase, and the parking lot packed with a thousand or more white trucks covered in mud. The fourth round had officially begun.

The first of the sets of clay pigeons exploded without a second thought, leaving nothing but an orange cloud drifting lazily on the breeze. Smoke rolled thick and acrid. He spun the empty gun on his finger like an old gunslinger, grinning wide enough to flash a gold tooth. The shotgun hit the ground, and a fraction of a second later, six playing cards came into view, fluttering into a high arc only a few feet away from where Hearst was standing.

Regardless of how Phoebe felt about the man, that son of a bitch drew fast, and he slapped the hammer of his golden Colt like he'd done it a million times before. He fanned the hammer in a blur—*crack-crack-crack-crack-crack-crack*. Paper shredded midair, holes punched clean through queens and kings and aces, and the cards landed into the dirt softly. Each one had a smoking hole right through the center, and the crowd ate every bit of it up. There wasn't a single detractor among them by the time he finished with the playing cards.

Last up was the glass ball. The crowd leaned in a little closer when Hearst picked up his rifle and pressed it against his shoulder. For reasons that only became clear after he started squeezing the trigger, he was relying on that same 6.5 Creedmoor to take a fifty-yard shot against the glass ball. In a series of motions as fluid as when he fanned his revolver, he fired a bullet at the dirt right in front of the glass ball, rocketing it up into the air more than a dozen feet high. The bolt slammed back and jammed another round in the chamber before the glass ball could even begin its descent, then became nothing more than dust in the breeze in the blink of an eye. It was all so perfect, flashy, and downright infuriating.

Brad was next. The crowd fell silent as the veteran stepped up. Brad was no show, no spectacle, just a singular, unflinching purpose. His own Remington 870 would be the shotgun taking on the clay pigeons. It was a plain pump that looked like it had seen real work in its day. He planted that prosthetic leg firm in the dirt and leaned into his shotgun before giving the signal that he was ready. The clays flew, Brad racked the gun and fired without hesitating. A shotgun cried out much sooner than Hearst's shot, and the twelve-gauge bird-shot left nothing but dust in its wake. There wasn't even a single wasted motion, just smoke curling slow from the ejection port.

He was just as deliberate when it came to the revolver portion. His Ruger hung big and mean at his hip. When the cards were flung into the air, he yanked out the revolver and fanned slow and steady, blowing holes into each and every card with surprising precision, like he was writing his name in lead. When he stopped after only firing five bullets, the crowd gasped in shock that he'd missed, but when the assistant lifted them up for the drones to capture, they saw he had fired a single bullet through the final two cards. The last bullet came as a surprise. Brad took a moment to do something uncharacteristic, he flaunted his skill with the revolver. As the assistant held up the stack of cards for the crowd to see, Brad let loose the last round, sending a .45 bullet through all six at once.

As the laughs and applause broke out, Brad holstered the revolver and kept moving. He lifted up the same rifle he'd been using and planted his leg once again, leaning into the stock pressed against his shoulder.

Phoebe wasn't sure if her eyes were lying to her, but before Brad could fire his first shot, she noticed that his prosthetic leg had snagged on a rock just a few inches too big around to give him a proper footing. Her jaw fell slack.

Brad squeezed the trigger, and the recoil sent him off balance. Because of that, the dominoes fell just as they had been set up. The glass ball shot up into the air, Brad yanked at the bolt to chamber a new round, and everything else turned into nothing but disaster. His prosthetic leg gave way, his weight shifting in the worst way, and his knee locked up. He stumbled back as the glass ball began to fall back to the earth, just as the veteran began to lose his balance and do the same thing his target was doing, and he frantically squeezed off one more round in the final hopes of a stroke of luck.

There was none to be found, though. The range officer's flag shot up red before he could pick himself up off the ground.

The arena exploded. Boos rained down thick as hail, mixed with cheers from folks who didn't like the quiet vet anyway. Arguments broke out in the stands with folks yelling it was the leg, not the man, others shouting rules were rules, and everyone letting the realization sink in that Brad had just been eliminated. The veteran just looked at the officer a long second, face carved from oak, then nodded once and walked off slowly. The prosthetic leg clicked unevenly the whole way, like it was arguing with the ground itself.

Phoebe felt it in her gut. The man had shot perfect time and time again and had been taken out by the very thing that kept him standing. The crowd quieted uneasily, like they'd seen something sacred broken.

Butler's turn was next. He looked worn thin, eyes shadowed deeper than yesterday's exhaustion. No magic Winchester to hide behind, just borrowed guns that didn't whisper sweet nothings at every target they were aimed at. He looked more like a hostage being forced to go through the motions than a competitor looking for a win. Even so, he was a man who knew his way around a firearm, and the three-gun challenge wasn't near as difficult for him as it should've been.

The shotgun split was clean but not flashy, smoke rolling slower than Hearst's, leaving a trail of orange dust wisping away until it was as invisible as the wind. He moved with an empty stoicism that fooled everyone but Phoebe, she knew it was nothing more than a guilty conscience. The cards fanned out next in a perfect display of ancient grace. Butler gently withdrew his loaner six-shooter and slapped the hammer six times to match the cards falling fast. His hand shook just a hair on the last shot, the holes were still good, but they were a far cry from the poetry he was known for. Within a few seconds, he was holding that Winchester again, and everything changed.

He smiled when he shouldered the rifle, the first

time anyone had seen that familiar smirk all day. He lifted the end of the barrel and wasted no time in squeezing the trigger. The glass ball shot up into the air, and a fraction of a second later, Butler yanked down on the lever and chambered another round. Before the glass ball could even reach its highest point, before gravity could even think about doing its job, Butler fired again, and the target shattered into a million pieces.

The crowd cheered this time just like they were hoping for. They unleashed a torrent of screams, chants, and celebrations for Butler, like they had just witnessed a historical event unfolding right before their very eyes.

Phoebe was last. She stepped to the line and the world narrowed—sun hot on her neck, dust in her nose, the weight of every eye pressing down like a hand on her chest. You'd think the crowd would be satiated after such a raucous for Butler, but they were eager for more. The announcer drew out long and dramatic—her name, the homestead girl, the one who shot a finger off a gunman, the Sure Shot who'd clawed through endurance with nothing but grit and a beat-up .22. The chant started low in the back rows and rolled forward like thunder across the plains.

"Sure Shot! Sure Shot! Sure Shot!"

Governor Rourke leaned on the rail of his box, Stetson gleaming, clapping slow but watching sharp as a hawk. He didn't join the chants for Phoebe, but when the screen flashed his face, Phoebe couldn't help but take in the look in his eyes—he was watching the fan favorite, whether he wanted to or not.

Phoebe went right to work, breaking the Parker open to get the round started. Its hinges creaked honestly just before two shells slid home fat and heavy. She snapped it shut, mounted the stock to her shoulder, and felt the pressure settle in. She nodded gently, and the clays launched with enough force to send two orange blurs streaking across the sky, crossing fast and high. Phoebe swung through the leader, trigger smoother than she ever thought it could be, and the recoil slammed against her shoulder. Orange dust bloomed just like a flower. Smoke hung thick, burned powder stinging her eyes, but both of those clay pigeons were damn sure gone.

The roar damn near shook the grandstands off their bolts. Next up, the revolver. Luck wasn't something she was typically used to, but for some reason, she was able to snag a genuine Colt revolver from the loaner rack.

It hung heavy at her hip. Her hands hovered steady over grips worn smooth by hands long dead and gone. She waited patiently for the playing cards, and even then, she was caught off guard when they came. Six cards tossed skyward, fluttering red and black against the blue sky in the background. Phoebe sucked in as much oxygen as her lungs could handle, yanked out the Colt from its leather holster, and thumbed the hammer.

Crack-crack-crack-crack-crack-crack.

The air filled with shredded paper, holes punched clean through the hearts and spades, cards drifting down ragged and ruined. They were still smoking when they hit the dirt. The last card, an ace of spades, even flickered with a small flame before dying out in the earth. The crowd lost its mind yet again.

Phoebe holstered the Colt and picked up the .22 that had gotten her this far. It was light, familiar, the one single piece of this madness that was truly hers. She was further away from the glass ball than she wanted, and the rifle she had most likely lacked the firepower necessary to launch the ball very high into the air. Her margins of failure were thin, and that meant she had to do everything exactly right, even perfect, if she hoped to move on.

She stepped to the mark, the crowd had gone hush except for the low thrum of expectation boiling. The glass ball mocked her in the distance, but there was nothing left to be done. Her only option was to do the impossible.

The .22 rifle shot out a bullet with a whimper compared to the other shooters, and the dirt exploded into the air less than an inch away from where the glass ball was resting. The next few seconds came as a blur to both Phoebe and the crowd hanging onto every movement captured by the fleet of drones swarming overhead.

The ball went only a few feet into the air, glinting in the sunlight just long enough for Phoebe to chamber the last round she'd need to move on. She went through the motions just like always, pulling the bolt back until the gentle click signaled the next bullet was ready to be chambered. She pushed the bolt forward again just before the glass ball began its descent, and her heart stopped.

The bullet had jammed into the feed ramp.

Panic rose to a lump in her throat, her heart sank to her belly, her hands froze, and her eyes glazed over. This was the end. She'd never make it to the next round if she didn't see that glass ball explode into pieces. She had to yank the bolt back, clear the jam, chamber another round, get the rifle back on target, and squeeze the trigger—all with enough time for the bullet to reach the ball before it hit the ground.

The world slowed until time itself completely stopped. Thoughts of her dad behind bars, her mom back home, and her future without them all flooded her brain, but there was no time to focus on anything but the task at hand. The .22's bolt was stove-piped. A rim-caught cartridge wedged sideways, the kind of cruel twist that happened once in ten thousand rounds but picked this moment, this shot, this heartbeat.

The crowd gasped in unison before falling silent, but Phoebe was already moving. Her motions were fueled by nothing but instinct. Her left hand slapped the bolt back, her right smacked the backside of the rifle, sending the wedged unspent round flying into the air. A fresh bullet popped up in its place to be chambered with a metallic snick that sang like pure salvation. Her shoulder took the recoil of the rack, cheek welded back to stock, front sight finding the falling ball through sheer muscle memory burned in from thousands of shots fired through the years.

The ball was an inch away from the ground, maybe less, when it shattered into a puff of red glitter and smoke, drifting out like fog on a winter morning. By the hair on her chin, she pulled it off.

The arena erupted louder than ever before with screams and hats filling the air, feet stomping the bleachers like thunder, and the drones doing everything they could to film the craze taking hold.

Phoebe lowered the rifle slowly, knees and elbows shaking violently from the surge of adrenaline. The jam had stolen seconds from her, precious, stupid seconds that put everything on the line.

With the crowd going wild and the governor

already settling into yet another speech highlighting the final three shooters who would be going on to the next round, Phoebe found herself looking down at her rifle with a tear welling up in the corner of her eye. She gripped the .22 Remington a little tighter, her eyes locked on the broken piece she was still holding onto. In the frantic second that her gun jammed, she forced the bolt forward so hard she'd actually snapped the charging handle smooth off of the gun, and that meant she couldn't chamber another round. It would have to be welded back on, or replaced entirely, and she didn't have either the time or money to do either of those things.

Her future in the *Texas Sure Shot* competition might've come to an end regardless of whether she hit the target or not. She dropped the split pieces of the rifle to the ground when the realization sank in, and a single tear streamed down her cheek as the crowd chanted her name over and over again.

Chapter 18

Some lies are so big they cast their own shadow, long and dark enough to swallow a man whole if he stands in them too long.

Butler knew those kinds of lies better than most. He'd been living in one for years, the kind built right on top of family tragedy with a rifle that wasn't rightfully his. After the three-gun round, the shadow of that long-held lie felt heavier than the Winchester case slung over his shoulder. He pushed through the canvas flap of the Bucket of Bullets tent saloon in desperate need of a drink strong enough to lighten that load, even just a little.

The place was packed tight, bodies pressed shoulder to shoulder under swaying lanterns that threw gold light across rough-sawn tables and faces already half-lit by cheap whiskey and cheaper talk. The air hung thick with cigar smoke, sweat, spilled beer, and the low rumble of voices swapping stories about the day's shooting—like it had been some kind of holy miracle instead of just men and women trying not to miss a single shot. A fiddler sawed away in the far corner, something fast and mean with a backbeat that matched the mood of folks still riding the high of clays exploding and glass turning to red smoke. Every stool was claimed, every inch of standing room taken by sunburned spectators in hats too big and boots too new, all of them reliving the moments they'd paid good money to see.

Butler worked his way to the far end of the plank bar, back pressed to the canvas wall, eyes on the flap like he was waiting for someone he both wanted and dreaded to walk through. He set the hard case down carefully between his boots, like the Winchester inside might decide to finally speak up on its own and force Butler to come clean about everything he'd done. Even through leather and padding, it felt hotter than the noon sun had been, burning a hole straight through to his conscience. He ordered a double bourbon—when he really wanted a whole bottle—while the noise washed over him and tried to drown out the day.

He was still tasting it all. The faint shake in his hand when he fanned those cards, the way the crowd had gone quieter for him than they had for her, the red smoke from Phoebe's glass ball hanging in the air like a judgment he couldn't outrun. He felt like he was trapped in those desperate few seconds stolen from Phoebe in a jam that should've, by all rights, ended her right then and there. Without her rifle in his hands, he'd scraped by. All he had to do was keep it for one more round, then he could fix everything.

He took a swig at the thought. The bourbon burned going down, familiar and unwelcome, but he welcomed it anyway.

Across the tent, Hearst held court like a king on a throne made of other men's fear.

The man had claimed the biggest table dead center, boots propped up on a crate, gold Colt laid out on the scarred wood like a trophy somebody else had bled for. A circle of drinkers surrounded him—sponsors flashing across neatly tucked in polo shirts, off-duty range officers, a couple of loudmouths in tactical vests nursing mugs of beer—hanging on his every word like he was about to give away every untold secret he'd ever kept from the world. His voice carried easily over the fiddle and the laughter. He was already one too many drinks in, cheeks flushed red below eyes bright with the kind of meanness liquor only sharpened.

Butler couldn't help listening. He knew Will Randy Hearst was a man who liked to hear himself talk, but even then, he couldn't help but pay attention to the vitriol he was spewing.

"...and don't even get me started on that little homestead girl," Hearst drawled, stretching the words slowly like it was an insult. "She thinks she's some kinda folk hero. *Sure Shot*, they call her. Real cute, ain't it? Crowd eats it up like she's a regular gunslingin' outlaw. But blood don't lie, y'all. I'm here to tell you one thing is for certain. Her daddy's rottin' in prison for damned good reason."

A few heads turned toward Hearst's table. A couple of nervous laughs rippled out, the kind men give when they're not sure if the joke's on them yet. Butler's grip tightened on the glass until his knuckles went white.

Hearst leaned forward, elbows planted wide, cigar glowing like a coal between his thick fingers. "Folks think it was just drugs or some petty robbery. I've even heard bullshit lies that he's an innocent man, wrongfully thrown in jail by a bunch of no-good badge-totin' oppressors. When have we heard that one before, right? Well, the truth's a lot uglier than that. Phoebe's dad got in too deep with a cartel operatin' out in the piney woods, believe it or not. They was stockpilin' illegal weapons, drugs, even women. We're talkin' sedition, plannin' who-knows-what against law-abidin' citizens and the government that keeps 'em safe.

"I was there when the sting went down. I saw the arsenal myself. There were crates of guns and explosives, makeshift cages crammed full with women and even children, and more drugs than a Colombian boat comin' to the States. Her old man was right in the middle of it, swearin' he'd die before he let anyone take what was his. Phoebe might tell you she's a saint, but I'll tell you what, she's anything but."

The tent got quieter, like someone had turned down the volume on the whole world. Even the fiddler eased up on the bow, notes trailing off into nothing. Butler felt ice crawl down his spine and pool cold in his gut. He knew the real story, the truth about what had happened. He knew exactly what Phoebe carried like a scar. Her dad was nothing more than a scapegoat, a man who found himself in the wrong place at the wrong time, but nothing like what Hearst was painting.

All it took was testimony from men who'd cut deals to save their own hides, men who most likely were on a first-name basis with Will Randy Hearst. Phoebe's dad was a man railroaded by bad evidence and worse ambition. But Hearst was twisting a quiet hunter who taught his daughter to shoot squirrels clean into some kind of domestic terrorist.

He took another swig of his bourbon, grateful that Phoebe hadn't arrived at the saloon with the rest of the shooters to hear Hearst's nonsense.

A drunk at Hearst's table barked a laugh, sloshing beer on his wrist. "So you're tryin' to say the apple don't fall far from the tree, huh? Girl's out here shootin' like she's provin' somethin'."

Hearst's smile was all teeth and no warmth. "Exactly right. And if she wins this thing—if the governor hands her that executive order on a silver platter—she'll use it to spring him. She will force this great state to put a drug runnin' maniac back out on the streets, let a dangerous man walk free so our sons and daughters can pay the price. That the Texas y'all want? Criminals walkin' free 'cause their daughters shoot pretty?"

Murmurs rippled outward now, uneasy and growing. A few hard nods from the tactical-vest crowd. A couple women shifted uncomfortable, eyes darting back and forth. Butler's stomach turned as he fought back the urge to stand up and say something, to defend the woman he'd known since he was just a child. But he didn't. He sat there drinking his bourbon without a single word escaping his lips. No matter how much he thought he'd changed through the years, he was coming to terms with the fact that he was that same little boy holding a rifle that didn't belong to him, deciding that it wasn't his job to do what was right.

Then Hearst leaned back in his chair, took a long pull on his cigar, and blew a lazy ring of smoke toward the lantern light overhead. "'Course," he said, voice dropping low enough that folks had to lean in to catch it, "if I win, I'll use that order mighty different."

Hearst let his promise hang there, thick as the

smoke, before providing the explanation that everyone in the Bucket of Bullets was hoping for, except for Butler.

"There's hundreds still locked up from that old sting. Some were guilty as sin, sure, but plenty of innocent bystanders too. Collateral, you might say, a necessary sacrifice to get the real bad ones off the street for good. If you hear about why I'm out here, you might hear that all I wanna do is lock more up, put more on track for the death penalty, and ruin the lives of those poor innocent *criminals*. But if you ask me directly, I'll tell you that I'm here to save the state of Texas. Plain and simple."

He looked around the table, ensuring to make eye contact with each of the drunks still listening. Hearst let a devilish grin overtake his face, like what he was really trying to say didn't need words. The tent went dead still. The fiddler's bow sawed back and forth to no end, punctuating the silence with a haunting screech that barely resembled a melody.

The tent suddenly became suffocated with air thick as tar mixed with molasses. Butler took a deep breath, trying to keep himself calm. He'd known Hearst was bad. He smelled it on him from the train ride, seen it in the way he stared at Phoebe, but this was pure rot clear through to the bone. The man wasn't just ambitious or mean—he was evil.

Hearst wasn't finished. He tapped ash onto the dirt floor deliberately, voice dropping even lower. "Truth is, that little girl has me to thank for who she grew up to be. I was the one who helped to put her old man away for good."

A couple men blinked. One leaned back like he'd been slapped. The table was quiet now and stayed that way until one drunk muttered something about going too far beneath his breath. Another shifted his chair back an inch. Hearst just grinned wider, like their discomfort was dessert.

"That's the difference between me and that little homestead girl. She wants mercy for one guilty man who'll probably go right back to plottin' against every single one of us good folks. I want justice for thousands. Texas needs a hard cleanin'. And *I'm* the goddamn broom."

Butler set his glass down hard enough that the bar rattled and bourbon sloshed over his knuckles. Heads turned his way, but he barely noticed. He was halfway to standing, blood roaring in his ears, when the tent flap burst open, and a kid in an orange event vest shoved through, sweating and out of breath, eyes wide.

"Phone call for Miss Phoebe Anne!" the kid shouted over the hush. "Governor's office. Urgent. They said now."

The tent erupted in whispers, sharp and sudden as buckshot. Hearst's table went dead quiet, his grin slipping half an inch for the first time all night.

Butler sank back slowly onto his stool. His hands shook worse than they had on the revolver stage that afternoon. The Winchester case sat at his feet like an accusation carved in walnut and steel.

Phoebe hadn't made it to the Bucket of Bullets saloon yet, she'd stayed on the line long after the scores posted. The last thing Butler saw was the color leaving her face when the armorer confirmed her .22's charging handle was sheared clean off, unfixable overnight. Butler had watched from the shadows, unable to find the words to intervene, then slunk away before she could spot him and see what was written on his face.

Hearst recovered his composure and let the news wash over him before raising his glass with a laugh that didn't quite reach his eyes. "Well, now. Looks like she's gonna get her fifteen minutes early, or maybe, if the governor's got the stones to tell her the truth, he's gonna break the bad news gently about her old man."

A few drunk laughs answered him, thinner than before. The mood had shifted subtle but sure. Folks glanced at each other uneasy, the weight of Hearst's words settling heavy.

Butler didn't join the laughter, he just sat there boiling in his own ineptitude. He stared at the bourbon he hadn't touched again, at the amber light catching in the glass just right as he swirled it around. He thought about every impossible shot he'd ever made with the rifle at his feet, about the sponsors watching, the contracts, the empire built on smoke and mirrors, and that same girl's legacy who had more enemies than friends in this world. He thought about Phoebe's face when the jam cleared and the glass ball burst, then about how that face turned sour when she saw what happened to her only gun. There was only one conclusion he could come to, and it was the one he wanted so desperately to avoid—Hearst couldn't be allowed to win.

The tent noise faded to a dull roar in his ears. The fiddler started up another tune, slower now, something minor and mournful. Outside, somewhere in the dark between tents and lanterns, Phoebe was taking a call from the most powerful man in Texas.

Butler didn't know what was being said, but he didn't need to. He knew whose side the line had just been drawn on, and for the first time in years, he knew which side of it he was going to stand on. Even if the light on the other side burned everything he'd built straight to the ground.

It was time to step out of the shadow he'd been hiding in.

Chapter 19

Some nights, the dark doesn't just fall. It rises up from inside you before the sun ever sets, slow and stifling, until it's all you can taste, all you can breathe, until it coats your lungs and makes every heartbeat the struggle of a lifetime. When night finally comes, it's all you can do not to wither away entirely.

Phoebe felt it rising deep in her stomach as she sat alone on the same overturned crate behind the chuck-wagon tents where she'd eaten cold brisket the night before and listened to an old drunk spin stories about the history books come to life again.

The fairgrounds were mostly quiet, just the low hum of generators winding down for the night and the occasional burst of laughter drifting from the Bucket of Bullets saloon across the way like smoke from a fire she wasn't invited to. The big lights were off, leaving only scattered security floods that painted everything in sickly sodium yellow and long black shadows that stretched farther than they had any right to. Brass still glittered in the dirt like scattered stars nobody had bothered to wish on, except for Phoebe.

Her .22 lay across her lap, broken clean in two places. The charging handle sheared off slick as if it had been cut deliberately with malice, the bolt carrier scarred and twisted from the force she'd used clearing that jam in front of God and governor and half the state. The armorer had shaken his head slowly when she'd brought it to him after the scores posted, he said it couldn't be fixed tonight. Parts would have to be ordered, a gunsmith would have to be hired, and it would all have to be paid for with money Phoebe simply didn't have. Tomorrow's final round was nothing more than a nightmare she couldn't escape from at this point, and she was still trying to find the guts to admit it to herself.

She turned the pieces of what remained of her only rifle over in her hands slowly, feeling the familiar weight gone wrong and hollow and meaningless. The rifle that had carried her this far in the competition—through lean winters and squirrels shot clean for supper, through drunks with bad intentions and impossible targets set by men who wanted to watch her fail—was dead in her lap. And with it, the last scrap of hope she'd been clinging to in order to free her dad from the jail that had kept them separated most of her life.

Without the .22 tomorrow, there was no hope of competing. She could beg and plead for a loaner, but those were only provided on rounds that required more than the rifle she brought herself. There was no guarantee that a borrowed gun would even be provided, much less one that could pull off whatever insanity the governor had conjured up for the final round of the *Texas Sure Shot.*

There was only one thing certain in her mind—she was done.

The crate creaked under her as she shifted, the sound loud in the quiet. Her whole body ached deep, her shoulders were knotted tight from recoil and tension, fingers raw and blistered inside the gloves, knees stiff from standing all day in heat that tried to cook her from the inside out. The ache in her chest was worse, though.

The phone in her pocket had buzzed three times while she walked back from the line, flashing the same unknown number on the screen. She'd ignored them all, lost in her own spiraling thoughts and unable to snap back into reality. It buzzed again, but this time she didn't even bother to look at it. Before she could return to her own wallowing, a boy in a bright orange vest popped up behind her like he'd just appeared out of nowhere.

"You Phoebe?" he asked in a rush.

"Who's asking?"

"It's for you." He shoved a cell phone into her chest, waiting just long enough for her to grab it before running away as quick as he'd shown up.

She hesitated to put the phone to her ear, wondering who might be trying to get in touch with her, and why it was urgent enough to have a kid like that running around looking for her at night. She swallowed once and lifted the phone.

"Miss Phoebe Anne?" The voice had come through coy and smooth at first, familiar from a hundred TV ads and her own time in the competition. "This is Governor Rourke."

Her mouth had gone dry before the governor

finished introducing himself. She'd managed to squeak out a response. "Yes, sir?"

He'd started easy, first congratulating her on making the final three, before going on a surprisingly lengthy story about how the people loved an underdog story, how she'd been the most impressive shooter in the competition, and how he still hasn't forgotten about how she saved him back at the opening ceremony. He said he'd been watching the feeds close, seen the crowd chanting her name and her own begrudging response to her rising popularity with the fans.

She'd stood there in the dark, heart thumping hard enough to hurt, thinking maybe this was it, the call that could change everything in her life. The one where he said her dad's case had come across his desk, that he'd looked at the files himself, that, as a favor for saving his life, he was ready to release her dad and let her get back to living her life.

That wasn't what the governor had in mind, though. His tone shifted cold, sharp as a skinning knife dragged slow across hide waiting to be yanked free of muscle and tendons and organs.

"But let's talk plain, miss. This competition's bigger than any one shooter. It's about Texas. About the image we put forward. This ain't what you wanna hear, I know, but Butler's the face we need. He's clean-cut, marketable, the kind sponsors line up for and networks love. You understand what I'm sayin', don't you?"

If Phoebe was being honest with herself, she had no clue what he was talking about. She had only just started to put the pieces together that this wasn't any sort of congratulatory phone call, it was something else entirely. When she couldn't find the words to answer, the governor just kept talking.

"I wouldn't go so far as to say you're distractin' from what we're tryin' to accomplish here, but you are becomin' a thorn in my side. Folks gettin' ideas about mercy for criminals because of your story, chantin' your name instead of his. That don't sit right with me, or those voters who put me in office. So, I guess you could say I'd like to pluck that thorn right here and now."

His words landed like they were the governor's own bullets, puncturing what little remained of Phoebe's wellbeing. They left her distraught, and the governor wasn't done yet.

"I know about your dad," he'd gone on, voice flat now, all the honey scraped off. "I got to know his file real well these last couple of days. Looks like he got mixed up in some real bad stuff, and now he's payin' the price. I bet you didn't know he was the victim of a sting operation, right? That he went behind bars with about a hundred other people, some of whom are still tied up in the courts. Those cases could go either way, if you know what I mean."

"I'm sorry, Mr. Governor," she spat out. "I don't understand."

"I mean, if you could help me out, maybe I could push for a new trial. It'd be quiet, no media circus. We could give your dad a chance to walk if the evidence holds up under fresh eyes, a real chance."

Her breath had caught hard enough to ache, her stomach was twisting and turning, her heart had stopped beating, she was hanging on every word the governor said.

"You just gotta do one thing for me," he'd said just

soft enough to hide the threat. "I want you to withdraw from the competition, and I want you to do it tonight."

Silence hung between them over the cell phone. There was no breathing or protesting, no more questions, just emptiness. This stayed for a few awkward seconds before the governor broke the silence yet again.

"You can cite the rifle malfunction and save face. I don't really care what you tell the people. But you get out, and you let the real competitors finish this thing. Texas gets the champion it needs. Your poor old man gets his day in court again. Everybody wins."

The words had hit like a slap across the face. She didn't know why she shouldn't be considered a real competitor after all she'd done. She had shot better than the professionals with a gun most shooters wouldn't be caught dead holding, much less actually shooting. She'd beaten them at their own game, and this is what she was getting in return? Her face scrunched, and her eyes narrowed. The fear and anxiety in her belly were burning away, leaving only furious rage inside her.

Over the next few seconds that ticked by like hours, she'd listened to him drone on about optics and the greater good, about how sometimes sacrifices had to be made for the state, how cooler heads needed to prevail, and a million other iterations of the same saying. He even went as far as to claim he admired her grit, truly did, but also that grit didn't keep people safe at night when they were cozy in their beds.

The threat hung there plain as the sun that would surely rise the next morning. It was thinly veiled in all the words the governor was throwing at Phoebe, but no matter how long that man kept talking, all she heard was just one thing. She had to quit.

"Think about your family, miss," he said, snapping Phoebe back to the man's voice in her ear. "Think about what's best for Texas."

Before she knew what happened, she'd pressed end without offering the governor even a single word in response. Her thumb pressed gently on glass until it went dark and she stood there until the phone went cold in her hand and the shakes set in. She found herself still sitting there on the same crate, still turning the broken pieces of her rifle over and over, feeling the rage boil until it threatened to overflow.

The thoughts swirling in her head were centered around the promise of a new trial for her dad, one where maybe he could see the light of day again. The only problem was that she knew how the last one went. Although she was too young to catch a whiff of the cooked reports and lies spewing from the stand, she knew the results better than anyone else. Another trial would just be the same old song and dance, and she'd be right back where she started, trying to undo the past.

The crate creaked again as she leaned forward, elbows on knees, broken rifle cradled like a corpse draped across her lap. Her whole body hurt, but the hurt inside was deeper, the kind that made you wonder if morning was worth waiting for or if the next breath was worth taking.

She was tired. Tired of fighting alone with nothing to her name. She was too exhausted by what her life had become since she decided to throw herself into the stupid competition that she gave real consideration to the governor's corrupt request to force her out of the

Texas Sure Shot. She knew deep down she'd be left with nothing if she accepted his offer. The distrust of people. Institutions, like what Governor Rourke represented, were born inside her the morning she lost her dad, and it would never be healed. She could never bring herself to trust a single word they offered, but she was also running out of options.

Without the .22, she had nothing tomorrow but empty hands. Hearst would chew her up slow and spit her out for the cameras. Butler would either coast on whatever he had left or win clean and prove once again that his only way forward in life was by spitting on the grave of her family's legacy.

Either way, her dad would stay locked up, her mom would keep gardening rocks, and Phoebe would return to that same patch of woods that gave them less and less to eat when dinnertime rolled around each night.

The only thing she could do now was give up. In fact, she was starting to think the governor's offer might be the only good thing to come of her efforts. It was a horrible thought to consider, but she could take him up and withdraw tonight. She could accept it before he changed his mind. All she had to do was call back, say yes, bow out gracefully, and maybe her dad really could get a fair trial. At least that would give him a chance, because from where she was sitting now, it seemed like the only chance she could give him. As much as she hated to even hear the thoughts in her head, there was one truth that she couldn't escape.

Quitting would be easier.

Her thoughts then drifted to a life she'd never known. She pictured what it would be like to pack up her meager bag and slip out before dawn, hitching rides all the way back home. There were no crowds chanting a name she didn't recognize, no pressures of every bullet being life or death, and no awkward, hateful clashes with Butler. She could finally see her family together, finally feel whole again. She could watch her mom and dad continue building their lives together, and for the first time in her entire life, she even allowed herself to imagine what it would be like to build a life for herself.

Butler came back to her thoughts and she shifted uncomfortably. He'd taken so much from her, and from a certain point of view, he could be blamed for everything she'd gone through. She knew better than anyone that it wasn't his fault that her dad was locked up so long ago, but what he took from her was the one thing her dad left that could take care of her and her mom. Butler stole their security, and in doing so, stripped them of a future they couldn't even dream of at this point.

Even so, in this picturesque life where all her problems had vanished, Butler was still there. He still had a way of popping up when she least expected it, or even desired it. She wanted nothing to do with him, but on the other hand, for reasons she didn't want to be truthful about, he still came to mind.

It was in this moment, sitting on the same old abandoned crate with the broken rifle in her lap and the phone still in her hand, that she had the worst idea she'd ever had in her life. Before giving Governor Rourke his answer, before gracefully bowing out of the competition, she wanted to talk to him one more time. Before she could allow herself to quit, she had to do the one thing she never wanted to do in a million years.

She had to ask Butler for help.

Chapter 20

What was she supposed to say? How would he react? Why would she expect him to be different this time?

The questions repeated over and over in Phoebe's mind. Butler had made his position known several times, claiming he was bound to people who owned him, that the rifle really wasn't even his to hand over. She'd let him wallow in his own self-pity long enough. If her situation was going to change, if she was actually going to shoot down the governor's offer, she was going to need her rifle.

The only problem was the sinking feeling that she already knew what Butler's response would be. In the furthest part of her mind, she could hear Butler's long-winded explanation. It would amount to nothing more than the simple fact that he only cared about himself.

Phoebe felt it deep now, walking the fairgrounds with the phone still cold in her pocket and the taste of the governor's threats thick on her tongue. She couldn't escape the thought that her only option was as futile as trying to shove another bullet in her broken

Remington. The call with the governor had ended minutes ago, but the words clung like burrs buried into her skin. She'd hung up without a word, stood there in the shadow between trailers until the shakes set in, then started moving because standing still felt like drowning.

The .22 pieces were back in her scabbard, broken and useless, clinking soft with every step like a reminder she couldn't outwalk. The fairgrounds had gone quiet, generators coughing their last sputters before fuel would inevitably run out, lanterns were already winking out one by one.

Phoebe wasn't wandering through the grounds aimlessly. At this time of night, there was only one place that allowed people to gather and fight and cuss each other out. She knew exactly where Butler would be—the Bucket of Bullets.

The makeshift tent saloon glowed faint across the way, canvas walls lit from inside like a campfire in fog. Laughter spilled out when the flap opened, then swallowed again. She pushed through without thinking, the warm air hitting her like a wall. It was the worst combination of cigar and cigarette smoke, spilled whiskey, sweat, backed up by the low twang of a fiddle winding down for the night.

Heads turned when she walked in, but she didn't pay them any attention. There were a few nods, a couple whispers, and plenty of eyes staring in her direction. She ignored them all as her eyes scanned the dimly lit tent until she found the man she was looking for at the far end of the plank bar, back to the wall, bourbon untouched in front of him. The Winchester case sat between his boots like something alive and waiting.

Butler didn't look up until she stopped right in front of him. His face was half shadow, half lantern gold, eyes carrying weight heavier than the case. He looked like a man who'd been drinking with ghosts and had forgotten who was even real. His eyes were empty.

Phoebe didn't speak. Instead, she pulled out the stool beside him and sat, the broken .22 scabbard clunking soft against the bar. The bartender drifted away the moment she sat down. Surprisingly, it was Butler who decided to speak first. His voice came low, rough as gravel.

"Heard about the rifle."

She let out a breath that might've been a laugh if there'd been any life left in it. "Whole state's probably heard by now."

He nodded slowly, eyes on the bourbon. "Also heard the governor called you."

It wasn't a question. Phoebe stared at the bar top, scarred and sticky from too many drunks who didn't know how to act. "Yeah," was all she could muster.

Silence stretched thick, the kind packed with years of things unsaid. Butler shifted, his boot nudging the case. "There's somethin' I gotta tell you," he started.

"I was gonna say the same thing."

They sat in silence, quietly debating which one should be the first to break the ice. Phoebe tried desperately to find the words to convince him to give up everything in his life, just so she could hold her own rifle again. On her way to the saloon, she had her entire speech planned out, word for word. But now that she was sitting in front of Butler, she couldn't find a single word. It was like her jaw couldn't even open, and her lips couldn't go through the motions anymore. All she could do was stare straight through him.

The fiddle sawed away in the background as mugs clattered and men grumbled beneath their breath. There was only the stench of regret and their own awkwardness that lingered between Phoebe and Butler. For a split second, they were finally kids again, looking at each other in the eye, free from the weight of their life's decisions and how it left one another feeling destitute in their own way.

Somebody laughed a little too loud at the other end of the saloon, and for reasons they couldn't explain, it spurred them both to speak up at the exact same moment.

"Listen, I—"

"I wanted to tell you—"

"You go first," said Butler.

"No," Phoebe answered without breaking eye contact. "I think it'd be better if you went first."

"Okay," he said before taking one last swig of his bourbon, swallowing so loud Phoebe could hear the gulp. "I've never been all that great with words, or really anything for that matter. So, I won't try to make up some long speech and go into a big ol' apology."

"Apology?"

Butler stopped for a second, then set his drink down and reached for the case resting at his feet. "Here," he said as he lifted the case holding Phoebe's Winchester. "This is yours. It always has been. And I am sorry about not givin' it back before today. I was wrong."

Phoebe looked at the rifle case in his hands and her heart stopped beating again. It was everything she hoped for, and she didn't even have to ask for it. Her trembling fingers reached out without a second thought and wrapped around the barrel and stock through the case. Its weight in her grasp brought her back to standing at the tree line years ago, seeing the cop car in the driveway on the horizon, the moment where her life would be changed forever. She could feel the wind blowing through the pines, hear the soothing words from Butler when he was just a boy, promising he'd give it right back as soon as it was safe. She could see her father being hauled away all over again.

"I don't know what to say," she finally let out.

"Not much to be said, I guess."

"Thank you, Butler."

"That's enough for me," he told her. "But it shoulda happened a long time ago."

"Yeah," she admitted. "It should have. You came around though, and I wasn't too sure you ever would."

"There's somethin' else..." His voice trailed off.

Phoebe couldn't take her eyes off the gun in her hands. It was like she was hypnotized by what she never thought she'd hold again. Her entire family's legacy boiled down to this one act, this one moment, and for a fleeting few seconds, she felt whole again.

Butler always did have a unique way of derailing her life, though.

"Hearst was runnin' his mouth again earlier. He said a lot of stuff you wouldn't care too much to hear," he explained.

"What else is new? That man has hated me from the start."

"There's a reason for that."

"What do you mean?"

"He knows about your dad," said Butler.

"Everyone does. The whole world knows about my problems now."

"No, not like that. He says he's known about it for

a long time, even claims he was behind the sting operation that got your dad put behind bars."

"What the—"

"I don't know if he's bein' honest or not, but he says that he's gonna use the executive order to keep him there as long as possible. Phoebe, he wants people like your dad to die in prison, sooner rather than later, too."

"That son of a bitch."

"Yeah."

Phoebe's stomach twisted in knots over and over again until she couldn't even breathe right. She hadn't heard it directly, but there was no reason not to trust what Butler was telling her at this point.

"It actually explains a lot," said Phoebe as she looked at Butler and nudged his glass. "Do you mind?"

"Be my guest."

Phoebe grabbed his bourbon and took a swig large enough to empty the glass. She waved down the bartender, who was doing his best to ignore them, and focused her attention back on Butler.

"He sent some guy to me before this thing ever kicked off," Phoebe started her own explanation. "I thought he was doin' it to everyone who wanted to join, thought he was just some competitive asshole that was tryin' to get a leg up."

"What do you mean he sent a guy?"

"He had some guy pull a gun on me and threaten me to stay home. He said I had no business competin', that it was better off if I just kept my mouth shut and didn't show my face."

"What did you say?"

Phoebe just stared at Butler, letting her eyes do all the talking.

"You didn't kill him, did you?"

"Come on, Butler, when have I ever gone that far? I only shot one finger off. I was bein' nice."

"That's one way to put it."

"Anyways," she tried to move on. "I think this whole thing is bigger than just Hearst. I can't prove anythin', but that phone call from the governor wasn't to congratulate me."

"What did he want?"

"Same thing Hearst wanted, for me to quit."

"That son of a—"

"Right?"

Phoebe looked at him then, really looked. She saw the lines the years had carved deep, the slump in the shoulders of the boy who used to run barefoot through pine thickets beside her. She saw the boy who'd missed squirrels on purpose just to watch her shoot, who'd held her hand the day the sheriff came. She saw the man who'd carried her legacy like a crown he hadn't earned, and she watched all the bravado, ego, and pretentiousness fade away until there was only concern in his eyes.

"I ain't askin' forgiveness," he told her. "I know I don't deserve it. I never did. But I can't stand by anymore. Not with Hearst fixin' to do what he's plannin'. Not with the governor danglin' your family like bait in front of a trap."

Her throat closed up tight. Tears stung hot suddenly, but she blinked them back and kept her focus on Butler.

"With this, you can win it all." He patted the gun case in her lap as he spoke.

She lifted it slowly, cradled it like something sacred had come home after too many years lost. The weight settled perfect against her palm, familiar as her own heartbeat. The saloon noise faded to nothing. Just the rifle and the man who'd finally brought it back.

"Thank you," she whispered through a cracking voice.

They sat there a long minute in the quiet, the rifle across her lap like a bridge built slow from years of wrong.

"I know the governor is lyin' to me," she said. "That's what politicians do. I know there ain't nothin' real about that man. But Hearst is different. If he wins…"

She didn't finish.

Butler leaned in closer, elbows on the bar. "We can't let him win."

"No, we can't," she agreed.

"But people like him, they don't quit."

"Same as the governor."

"We're gonna have to send a message, then."

"They ain't gonna listen, Phoebe. That's what I'm tryin' to tell you."

"This time they will." Phoebe looked down at the Winchester, fingers tracing the grain slow like reading braille. Her eyes came up sharp, glinting in the lantern light. "Because we're gonna use the only language people like that understand."

Butler's mouth twitched, the ghost of a smile that didn't reach his eyes yet. "I missed that look in your eyes." He leaned in closer, their heads coming together in the smoky light, voices dropping to whispers the fiddle couldn't drown. "What did you have in mind?"

"Here's what we're gonna do," Phoebe began.

Chapter 21

The next day came like a letter from the IRS, where crippling debt was due, and the collector had come for what was already theirs.

The sunlight burned off the night's thin haze until the fairgrounds just outside of Austin lay open and exposed under a sky that felt too wide, too blue, too honest for the kind of reckoning that was waiting. Smoke from the chuckwagons rose in lazy columns, mesquite and hickory curling into the still air, carrying the smell of brisket, ribs, pulled pork, and stuffed sausage that had been smoking since dawn and coffee so strong it could wake the dead.

The dirt road leading in was already choked with trucks and RVs, people who'd driven through the dark just to be here, hats tipped back, boots scuffing the ground, eyes bright with that peculiar Lone Star hope that says if something's impossible, it's only because a Texan hadn't tried it yet.

The state had turned the main arena into something that looked like a dream Buffalo Bill might have conjured up after too much whiskey and not enough sleep. Bleachers rose in steep tiers around a wide circle of packed dirt, red-white-and-blue banners strung between telephone poles that snapped in the breeze like flags at a funeral for something that hadn't died yet. A brass band was already working through "The Yellow Rose of Texas," the notes bouncing off the grandstand where the governor sat in a high-backed leather chair that looked like it belonged in the mansion he called home, thanks to the voters who put him there.

He wore a white Stetson and a smile that showed too many teeth, flanked by two state troopers who kept their hands near their holsters and a row of celebrities who'd been flown in for the cameras. There were plenty of names that everyone recognized in attendance. To the crowd, they were celebrities in every meaning of the word. A country singer with a voice like warm bourbon and a hat that cost more than most people's houses, a retired quarterback who kept adjusting his cowboy boots like they pinched, and an actress whose smile was practiced and perfect for the lenses that never stopped rolling. Influencers, oil tycoons, trust fund babies, and every other type of person with self-imposed importance surrounded them, giving just enough fuel to ignite the crowd wilder than they ever had been.

The place was a complete frenzy with laughter rolling through the stands, kids running between legs with cotton candy stuck to their fingers, old men in faded rodeo shirts telling stories about the last time something like this had come to Texas. Vendors hawked barbecue sandwiches and cold beer, and every few minutes a would-be cowboy would shout "Come and get it!" from the chuckwagons, sending a fresh wave of ribs and brisket into waiting hands. The air tasted of smoke and gun oil and the faint sweet burn of gunpowder from the warm-up rounds earlier that morning. Somewhere, a fiddle was sawing a slow, mournful tune, the kind that made you think of lost things and second chances.

Butler watched it all with a solemn look, like he was attending his own funeral.

Soon, all the pomp and circumstance would be gone, and he'd have to face down the people who gave him his empire. He'd have to admit to what he'd done, and ultimately, he'd have to give it all up. The thought shook him to his core, but there was something else deep down, something he still hadn't fully admitted to himself. The only thing he knew for certain was one simple fact. He was ready.

He stood at the edge of the shooting line, the empty Winchester case still slung over his shoulder. The night had passed in the back of his trailer with Phoebe right by his side, the two of them bent over the plan, whispering it over and over until the words stopped sounding impossible and started sounding like the only thing that could save them both. Now, he felt the weight of every eye on him, every camera lens, every sponsor who'd bet their money on him winning this thing clean and easy. He felt the governor watching too, that tight smile never quite reaching his eyes. He felt Phoebe standing twenty feet away, the Winchester in her arms now, barrel pointed at the sky, hidden in a case no one else would recognize. She didn't look at him. She didn't need to. They'd said everything they needed to say in the dark.

There were only three shooters left in the *Texas Sure*

Shot competition. Hearst, Butler, and Phoebe stood alone like inmates awaiting judgment. There was only one chance left for each of them. The announcer's voice rolled out over the loudspeakers, deep and theatrical, the kind of voice that belonged to old radio serials.

"Ladies and gentlemen, boys and girls, welcome to the final round of the *Texas Sure Shot*! Today, the last three shooters in the greatest marksmanship competition this state has ever seen attempt the most impossible shot ever devised in the history of the sport. You will not believe your eyes!"

The crowd roared, a wall of sound that rolled over the arena like thunder. They were already half-drunk on adrenaline and beer and the promise of something they'd talk about for the rest of their lives.

Downrange, three hundred yards away, the target waited like a promise of a better life. It was a small steel plate no bigger than a playing card, painted black so it swallowed light, barely visible to the naked eye. Behind the shooters was the real twist though—a mirror. This time, it wasn't the announcer's voice that broke through the noise, it was the governor's.

"You might've guessed it by now, but the final round is a homage to the greatest to ever do it. This trick may have been pulled off by legends before, but never at this range, and never under these circumstances!" The governor raised his voice to match the swell in the cheers and continued his speech.

"Each shooter will stand with their back to the target, facing the mirror with only its reflection to aim. That's right, this is the historic backward mirror shot seen in history books and told in tall tales, but never before done on camera! Welcome to the *Reverse Trick Shot!*"

Butler analyzed the target as the governor droned on and on. The plate was set at an angle that meant a perfect shot, hitting dead center of the steel, would ricochet safely into the dirt. It was simple enough, but also the kind of shot that most people would call impossible.

Butler's stomach twisted. He'd run the numbers in his head a thousand times. He knew what he had to do, and he knew what Phoebe had to do after him. There was a certain etiquette that could be predicted when it came to gun safety, and that was something the state itself couldn't shirk. There were too many lawyers, too many professionals, and too much money wrapped up in the competition to make it presentable to the world to afford anything less than perfection. The plan he and Phoebe had devised depended on it.

He couldn't help but think of how much he'd given away, and how little he'd get in return. He could still feel the grain of the Winchester against his palm from the night before, he could still feel the loss when he pushed it into Phoebe's chest, what he'd given up for the sake of her own future instead of his. He thought of the way her fingers had traced the wood, slow and deliberate. He thought of the way she'd looked at him in the saloon when he handed her the case, like she was seeing him for the first time in years, like she was seeing the boy who'd promised to keep the rifle safe and hadn't.

The announcer called the first shooter, interrupting his spiraling thoughts. He'd zoned out for the remainder of the governor's lengthy words of anything but wisdom.

"Hearst! Step to the line!"

This time, there was a mix of cheers and boos. Hearst had developed a reputation with the crowd, and that meant he was divisive. Some people seemed to really relate to the villain of the competition, a role that Hearst ultimately embraced wholeheartedly. He walked out like he owned the dirt, tall and lean in a black duster and a flat-brimmed hat, the kind of hat that looked like it belonged in a movie nobody wanted to watch. He carried a custom long-range .308 rifle with a suppressor that cost more than most people's houses. It was a gun he hadn't used at all in the competition, one that he clearly felt matched the weight of the event. Deep down, Will Randy Hearst was a showoff, and even he couldn't stop himself from flaunting for the crowd.

Butler watched in disgust as he got into position, coming face to face with the golden-framed mirror set up for the shooters. With the target at his back, he lazily lifted the rifle and let it come down on his shoulder, keeping his fingers gripped on the stock and his index pointing forward. He reached up and adjusted the mirror with a small nudge, urging the crowd into a new roar of cheers and boos before everyone in the festival fell silent. The only sound was the wind in the banners and his own breath, in and out.

Hearst soaked in all the attention, taking far longer than any man should, even for a shot of this magnitude. It may have just been a fun competition for those in attendance, but Butler knew what that man was really thinking. Hearst had placed the weight of the entire state on his own shoulders all by himself, and this was his chance to show what he was made of. The shot cracked sharp and clean. The bullet hit the plate dead center, sending the round into the earth with an explosion of dirt and rocks.

The crowd exploded. They'd seen something impossible, and they clearly loved it. The governor clapped politely, but his smile was tight. The celebrities cheered even though they didn't understand. The whole place acted like they'd just watched a final-second touchdown Hail Mary to win the Super Bowl—except for Butler and Phoebe.

Butler's mouth had gone dry watching Hearst make the impossible shot. For all the bitterness and hatred and conspiring, there was an undeniable skill that man possessed with a firearm. In a matter of seconds, the stakes became all too real. If Butler and Phoebe missed their shot, the competition had already been won.

He watched Hearst dust off his coat and give the governor a slow nod before turning to the crowd and jeering them in a way only he could. The man looked satisfied, confident even, like he'd already won the competition and could taste the executive order he'd use to keep Phoebe's father locked away. He was a man who looked like he was about to bend the entire world to his will.

Butler felt the old anger rise in his chest, the same anger that had been there since the night he'd taken the rifle and never given it back.

"Next shooter—Butler!"

The name hit him like a punch. He walked to the line to the tune of thousands of fans who loved him and everything he ever did. He listened to their adoration, knowing he was about to betray them all, just like he'd betrayed himself, but he didn't care. There was something else he cared about, something he still struggled to admit to himself, and in this out-of-body moment where he took his place at the final round of the *Texas Sure Shot* competition, he allowed himself to look at her one more time. It would be the last time he looked at her with regret in his eyes.

She looked back at him and smiled. His heart warmed over, and his fingers stopped trembling. His focus returned, and he did the only thing he could think of in the moment—he smiled back at her.

With steady hands and a heart hammering in his chest so hard he could feel it in his throat, he turned to face the mirror. Instead of trying to find the target, he just stared at himself. He didn't recognize the man staring back at him, and he couldn't have been more proud of that small fact. There was a lifetime's weight lifting from his shoulders as he stood there and basked not in the attention from the crowd, but his own reversal of a wrongdoing that never should've happened.

When he finally broke free of his own reflection, he found the target in the mirror with ease, and everything else fell right into place. He'd made harder shots a dozen times before, but not with the loaner .223 he held in his hands. It was a forgettable rifle, but the shot he was going to make would be anything but that. He lifted the rifle, coinciding with the swell in cheers from the crowd that died the very second the barrel of the gun came to rest on his shoulder.

It was an odd position to be in, facing away from the target you were trying to hit, holding just the stock without it butted up to a shoulder that could catch the recoil. Everything was backward and unnatural, meant to put each shooter in a position that was anything but intuitive. This is where pure, God-given skill would make the difference, and for the first time in as long as Butler could remember, he was nervous about squeezing the trigger.

He took a breath, and before letting it out, he allowed his finger to rest on the trigger. He eased it back until he could feel the trigger reset point, a small resistance where everything would hang in the balance. He thought of Phoebe standing behind him, thought of the night they'd spent going over this moment, thought of the boy he'd been in the piney woods and the man he'd become, and the man he was trying to be now. He thought of the rifle he'd carried for years, the one that had never missed, the one he'd refused to give back. He thought of the years he'd spent pretending he was something he wasn't. He thought of the way Phoebe had looked at him in the saloon when he handed her the case, like she was seeing him for the first time in years, like she was seeing the boy who'd promised to keep the rifle safe and hadn't. He thought of the way her voice had cracked when she thanked him and the three words he desperately wanted to tell her.

Then, he squeezed the trigger.

The shot exploded through the hush of the crowd, but instead of that sweet, ringing sound of steel, there was only a soft *thump* and an audible gasp from the crowd. The bullet had come a few inches too low, smacking the stand the target was welded to and just barely nudging the angle of the plate before the bullet was lost in the woods behind it. The angle had just barely changed, but not enough for anyone to notice unless they were looking for it.

The bell didn't ring. The crowd didn't cheer. The governor didn't smile.

A murmur rolled through the stands, confusion and disappointment mixing together. Butler stood still, facing the mirror and taking in the reflection of a new man, a man he could stand to look at. While the fairgrounds fell as silent as the grave, Butler calmly slung the rifle over his shoulder and walked back to the line without looking at anyone. He could feel Phoebe's eyes on him, steady and sure. They'd gone over it a hundred times.

The announcer's voice cracked with surprise. "Well, folks, that's a miss! Butler is officially eliminated!"

Boos rained down on the line of contestants, getting louder and louder. Some people were throwing trash onto the field, and others had already started to pack their bags to leave. The governor sat there without moving a muscle, his face saying everything that needed to be said.

All three shooters stayed lined up just like they were before, but only Hearst responded. His laugh was louder than the boos, like thunder coming from the distance before rumbling over everyone at the competition. It came from deep in his belly, exploding out with more power than any bullet, aimed directly at Butler.

He stood there without showing a sign of remorse, knowing every sponsor who owned him was watching closely. He let Hearst laugh in his face and the crowd curse his name. He let it all happen until the announcer deemed it appropriate to interrupt the shock of what had just happened.

"It's time for our final shooter—Phoebe Anne!"

It was like there was an entirely different crowd of

people in the stands when they heard Phoebe's name. Chants started almost immediately, and everyone joined in like it was a chorus to a song meant just for them. They'd been chanting her name all week, but now it was deafening, a wave that rolled over the arena like a storm breaking. Kids were jumping up and down. Old men were wiping their eyes. The brass band struck up again, faster now, almost frantic.

Butler watched Phoebe walk forward, putting one foot in front of the other, slow and steady. She didn't look at the governor, at Hearst, or even him. She just looked straight ahead, with the Winchester still slung over her shoulder, hidden in plain sight.

If anyone thought the gasp from the crowd was loud when Butler missed the shot that could've won the competition, they would soon find out just how loud they could really get when Phoebe pulled her rifle out. Those fans weren't stupid, and neither was the governor.

She lifted the Winchester out of the case, and the world went quiet. She was graceful with every motion, taking her time to set the case down and find her way to the line to take her shot.

Butler's throat closed up. He struggled to take each breath as he watched Phoebe take the stage at last. He saw beauty he'd never known before, a woman who had become the only important thing in his life after spending all his time running from her. He confronted everything he knew he should have been doing all along right then and there.

When Phoebe finally turned around to come face to face with the mirror that would guide her final shot, she gave the competition something she'd withheld through every round and every public appearance.

She looked at herself standing in the mirror, holding the rifle her dad gave her, and finally, she smiled.

Chapter 22

Everyone's favorite part of a wedding isn't the food or the reception, the music, or even the groom, it's when the bride first appears for her walk down the aisle.

The people in attendance make plans and gather their belongings, they prepare their family and loved ones, their clothing, their gifts, and they ensure to put their best foot forward for the ceremony. The groom is making the decision of a lifetime, one that he will never come back from, or at the very least, will be forever changed because of his choice. He stands waiting at the end of it all like he is awaiting a prize, but that isn't what finds him. What he finds is a future worth standing and waiting for, a relationship that makes him complete, and a family that is eager to grow twofold. The most climactic moment of such an event should be the union between them, the moment where the bride and groom finally touch lips to seal their fate, but that couldn't be further from the truth. What catches everyone off guard, what leaves everyone speechless, is the dramatic reveal of her in a wedding gown.

The sudden stillness that had fallen over the fairgrounds was no different than a church full of spectators eagerly waiting for the woman wearing a white dress to turn the corner and walk toward a fairytale ending. The brass band had stopped playing mid-note, the fiddle hanging in the air like a held breath. Barbecue smoke drifted lazy and thick, but nobody moved to eat. The vendors had frozen with their tongs mid-turn, the kids with cotton candy halfway to their mouths, the old men with their stories cut off in the telling. Even the wind seemed to have taken a back seat to what was about to happen. Everything had come to a complete halt, speechless in the reveal of what was in the hands of the girl who'd become known as *Sure Shot* herself.

Phoebe stood at the line with the Winchester steady in her arms, barrel still pointed skyward. She could feel the weight of every eye in the place, thousands of them, plus the drones swarming everywhere overhead, plus the governor's, plus Butler's. She didn't look at any of them. She looked at the mirror, at the small black steel plate three hundred yards downrange, at the skewed angle Butler had left behind with his miss.

She knew what the rifle could do. She'd known it since she was a little girl standing in the piney woods with her dad's hand on her shoulder, showing her how to hold the stock, how to breathe, how to let the shot be the only thing that mattered. The rifle had never missed, not once, and it wasn't about to start now.

She knew what would happen, just like everyone else in attendance. If she missed now, that rotten man standing in line with Butler would walk away with the win. He'd take the executive order and use it to keep her father locked up, maybe worse. The thought sat in her stomach like cold lead, but she didn't let it move her. She'd spent too many years letting other people decide what her life would be. Today was going to be different. Today, she'd do something she'd never done before.

The crowd watched, silent now, waiting for the miracle they'd come to see. Instead of lifting the Winchester, she reached down and shoved her hand into her pocket. Everyone at the event was hanging onto every movement, including the governor. When she pulled out a small, black bandana, everyone put the pieces together at the exact same time, and complete chaos ensued.

She folded the bandana a couple of times in her hands, then reached up and tied it behind her head, embracing the complete darkness that overtook her vision. She couldn't see the target anymore. She couldn't see the mirror. She couldn't see Butler or Hearst or the crowd or the sky. All she had was the memory of the angle, the feel of the rifle in her hands, and the certainty that the shot would find its mark. She could still hear the crowd losing their mind, though, and for a couple of seconds, she let herself imagine what the governor was thinking, what his face looked like when he saw her holding that Winchester. That wasn't what made her smile, but it was damn close.

Without looking at anything, she lifted the Winchester slowly, like it was part of her, like it had never left her hands for a single day. She rested it on her shoulder just as her finger found the trigger. Her breathing was steady, her grip firm, but none of that mattered, everything she was doing was simply for show. She exhaled and embraced the darkness through the blindfold. There, she could finally let her dad's words go through her mind one more time.

You can't miss if you only have one bullet.

As the crowd readied themselves for what was to come, she did what no one expected. At the bottom of her breath, she squeezed the trigger without a second thought. It took her all of two seconds to fire that round. She didn't bother to aim, think twice, or make the slightest adjustments to her posture, much less where the end of that rifle was pointing. All she did was get the rifle over her shoulder and squeeze the trigger.

It wasn't the suddenness of the gunshot that took the crowd by surprise, it was where the bullet went. One second saw the Winchester blasting out smoke and fire and lead, and the next saw only blood and bone and death.

The shot cracked out, echoing through the stands filled with people and the trees that surrounded them, and the bullet flew right as rain. It struck the steel plate dead center, but instead of bouncing back and slamming into the dirt like originally intended, it came right back in the direction it was fired from, all because of the skewed angle Butler had expertly left behind. Before Phoebe could take the blindfold off her face, she knew her bullet had found its target by the sounds of the crowd. Cheering and booing had turned to screams of panic.

The bullet had traveled three hundred yards to find the center of the steel plate no larger than a playing card before ricocheting and traveling three hundred yards back to bury itself right in the middle of Hearst's forehead.

He was lying dead in the dirt by the time Phoebe's eyes could adjust to the sunlight again. Amid the frenzy unfolding at the fairgrounds, people fleeing the stands, the drones closing in all around her, capturing what had seemingly turned into a crime scene, and the governor watching over his schemes going up in flames, Phoebe watched the last breath escape from Hearst's lungs.

She was still holding the Winchester when she started walking back to the lineup where the shooters had been forced to stand. One was dead, the other had lost it all, but she had won.

Instead of taking her place in the lineup, she walked up to Butler, coming within inches of him before stopping. His face was pale and his eyes wide, but there was something else, something unspoken between them. The roar of the crowd had turned destitute, the drones were scurrying around, and the governor was already retreating back to the shadows from where he came, but Phoebe and Butler remained, staring at one another.

She felt everything she'd ever felt for the man standing across from her come and go in an instant. The childhood adoration, the sting of his betrayal, the lingering hatred at his absence, and the flood of emotions that came when he finally did the right thing. She savored what it was like to feel things finally swinging in her direction, but she was never one to leave the world to its own vices. Finally, after all this time, she'd learned to go out and make a life happen for herself.

They were in their own world, one where Butler's was crashing down all around him and Phoebe's was finally coming back from the grave. Everything was going to change from here on out, that much was for sure, and even if most of it couldn't be controlled by either of them, there was one final thing they could control. Before his sponsors could take everything from him, before her dad would finally step free from behind the bars, there was one final thing between them that had to be resolved.

Butler's eyes were wet, shining with relief and fear and something neither of them had dared name until now. Phoebe stepped forward, slow and deliberate, until she was close enough to feel the heat coming off him. She looked up into his face. He looked down into hers. Neither of them spoke. The animosity that had stood in their way was disappearing by the second. The rifle was back where it belonged. And whatever came next—sponsors, governors, trials, cameras—they'd face it together.

The crowd's roar had turned into something else entirely now, a wave of sound that resembled the ocean off the coast of Galveston more than a thousand fear-stricken fans. Phoebe felt the vibration of it in her chest, but it didn't touch her. She could still smell the gunpowder clinging to her hair, the faint tang of barbecue smoke that had settled into Butler's shirt, the salt of sweat, and the sweetness of a day they had both carried for far too long. The chaos around them—the fleeing people, the buzzing drones, the governor's failure—felt distant and irrelevant.

Neither of them spoke. Instead, she reached up, cupped his face with both hands. The kiss was slow and sure, the way a promise should be. Everything else faded away into a blur.

There was only the two of them, the rifle still in her grasp, and the years that had finally fallen away.

Chapter 23

The thing about humans is we always want to see what's next, what lies around the next corner, what waits for us just over the hilltop.

For Phoebe and Butler, what awaited them was two never-ending white lines stretching out into the horizon. The road called their name, and they simply had to answer. The morning light that rose over the treetops filtered down in thin gold shafts that whispered forgiveness to anyone with eyes to see it. Each ray caught on the dust motes that hung in the air above the old dirt drive, turning everything they touched into something quiet and hopeful. The homestead looked smaller than Phoebe remembered, or maybe she was just bigger now. The garden her mother had tended through lean years was bursting with late tomatoes and okra, the rows straight and proud. The truck sat loaded in the yard, tailgate down, boxes and cases stacked neat and tight, ready for whatever road lay ahead.

Phoebe stood on the porch with a clipboard in her hand, pencil tucked just inside her hair behind her ear, going down the exhaustive list one last time. She'd gone over it a dozen times before, but every item on it felt like a promise kept. She'd written it out several nights before, sitting at the kitchen table with Butler across from her, the two of them quiet and easy in a way they hadn't been since they were kids running through these same woods that reached into the sky behind them.

Passports were already packed. Thick blue books with fresh pages waiting to be stamped in places she'd only ever seen on maps. Identification and itinerary were sorted and stored. A fat envelope of them, in fact, some with gold seals, some with red wax, all earned after weeks of paperwork and phone calls and favors traded in rooms she'd never thought she'd enter.

After giving up on the argument entirely, their costumes were tucked neatly away in their baggage. New, matching leather vests with patches stitched by a woman who'd watched the competition on television and cried when Phoebe won. They were simple but sharp, the kind of thing that looked good under stage lights without pretending to be anything they weren't.

She was holding the tickets in the clipboard, refusing to let them out of her sight. A thick folder of them made it difficult to actually write. They were first-class where it mattered, economy where it didn't, routes mapped out across oceans and continents like a trail of breadcrumbs leading them farther from home than either of them had ever been. They'd even taken out a special insurance policy on their road trip. The papers had been signed in triplicate, covering everything from lost luggage to broken bones to the kind of headlines nobody wanted to think about.

The list went on, each item crossed off with a firm

line that felt like closing a door on the past. Phoebe ran her finger down the page, making sure nothing had been missed. There was plenty more they'd have to get while on the road. Things like ammunition, something they'd need cases and cases of over the next few months, and even an assortment of props like steel plates, mirrors, and those cursed glass balls would all be waiting on them at each destination.

There was one thing missing, though.

The truck they were packing was overwhelmingly large, with an unfamiliar logo stuck onto both the driver and passenger side doors, reading *Nations Heritage & Culture Preservation.* It belonged to a couple who'd introduced themselves simply as Davy and Rose just a few months ago. They had been following Butler's rise to stardom and eventual downfall when he gave up the *Texas Sure Shot* competition for Phoebe to win. They didn't come empty-handed either. Davy and Rose were the new financiers, investors, producers, and fans of the show that Phoebe and Butler would be taking on the road for what seemed like the entire world to see.

Davy was a big man with a bigger laugh, the kind of laugh that made you feel like everything was going to be all right even when it wasn't. Rose was keen with sharp eyes that missed nothing and a smile that could cut glass when she needed it to. They'd bought into the tour outright with venues booked on damn near every continent. The couple had a whole speech planned about how everyone needed to see what Phoebe was capable of. Whether she actually believed it or not, they were adamant about it, and they had more money than she or Butler had ever seen to back it up.

There were promoters lined up who'd never seen

shooting like this and were willing to pay to be the first to. They called it the *Sure Shot World Tour*, and the posters were already printed. It was still difficult to imagine Phoebe taking center stage, Winchester raised, and the only man she could ever want at her side—Butler.

He came around the side of the truck, wiping his hands on a rag, sweat darkening the back of his shirt. He'd been checking the tie-downs, making sure nothing shifted on the long haul to the coast, where the ship waited. He caught Phoebe's eye and smiled. The sort of small, private kind of smile that belonged only to her now. She felt it in her chest, warm and welcoming.

"Did you find it?" she hollered out to him.

"Not yet," he said back to her. "It's probably already in the truck. Didn't you pack it first thing last night?"

"I thought you had it?"

"We'll find it, we'll find it."

Davy clapped his hands together, the sound sharp in the morning quiet. "That's the last of it, right?" he called, voice booming. "We're ready whenever you are, Miss Sure Shot."

Rose smirked, low and fond, leaning against the truck fender. "Don't rush her, Davy."

Phoebe folded the clipboard under her arm and walked down the steps. She couldn't leave without every single thing on the list, but she knew the time had come to say goodbye. The dirt was loose beneath her boots, the same dirt she'd run barefoot across as a child, the same dirt that had held her father's footprints before they took him away, but she'd never been as sure-footed in her life.

She stopped in front of her parents, close enough to see the new lines around her mother's eyes, the gray in her father's beard that hadn't been there before. Her mother reached out first, her fingers brushing Phoebe's cheek, then pulling her into a hug that smelled of garden soil and coffee and home. Her father's arms came around them both, strong and careful, like he was afraid she might break. Phoebe held on tight, breathing them in, letting the moment stretch until it felt like it would hold forever. When they stepped back, her father's eyes were wet, but he was smiling. He didn't say much these days, but his eyes followed Phoebe everywhere, soft and steady, like he was still making up for lost time.

Butler was waiting by the truck, door open, engine idling soft. Davy and Rose were already inside, giving them space. Phoebe turned back to the porch one last time, lifted her hand in a small wave. Her parents waved back, standing together in the doorway like a picture she'd carry with her everywhere she went, to every country and every city.

She climbed into the truck, settled into the seat beside Butler. He reached over, took her hand, and threaded their fingers together. Before the truck could pull away, she flipped to the last page of the clipboard one more time and read the final item, written in large letters, underlined twice, with several exclamation points. Butler leaned in close and chuckled.

"Still haven't found it?" she asked one more time, this time with even a hint of worry finding its way into her voice.

"You know how much I love finally bein' able to say this." He locked eyes with her. "I was right all along."

He lifted up a leather case with a gold zipper closed up tight around the Winchester—the rifle that couldn't miss, the one that once belonged to the real little Annie Sure Shot, the heirloom handed down from her father—and Phoebe exhaled a sigh of relief.

It was time to finally begin a life of her own.

A Look at: Western Fiction Ten Pack: Volume Two: Ten Full-Length Classic Westerns

TEN FULL-LENGTH WESTERN TALES OF GRIT, GLORY, AND GUNSMOKE.

A young man returns home to find his family slaughtered and sets out on a relentless path of revenge. A lawman with a notorious temper risks everything to see a brutal outlaw hang—even if it costs him his town. A park ranger stumbles into a high-stakes treasure hunt where bullets fly, alliances shift, and an empire's fate hangs in the balance.

From the windswept plains of Texas to the rugged peaks of Colorado, ten of the best Western authors take you on a ride through the untamed frontier, where justice is written in lead, and legends are born in fire. As these trailblazers battle deadly enemies, face impossible odds, and chase the promise of fortune, one thing is certain… not all will live to tell the tale.

The Western Fiction Ten Pack: Volume Two is an unforgettable collection of full-length, first-in-series novels packed with classic Western action. If you love hardened gunfighters, lawless frontier towns, and high-stakes showdowns, this box set is a must-read.

AVAILABLE NOW

A [illegible] Western Fiction
Ten Pack: Volume Two: Ten
Full-Length Classic Westerns

TEN FULL-LENGTH WESTERN TALES OF GRIT, GLORY, AND GUNSMOKE.

[illegible]

[illegible]

[illegible]

AVAILABLE NOW

Thank You

Thank you for taking the time to read *Sure Shot.* If you enjoyed it, please consider telling your friends or posting a short review. Word of mouth is an author's best friend and much appreciated.

Thank you.
Nicholas Osborn

About the Author

Nicholas Osborn is a second-generation ranch owner and storyteller from the heart of deep East Texas. With a career encompassing everything from entertainment marketing to news journalism over the last decade, he has studied the craft of authentic storytelling and honed his writing throughout the years.

Nicholas's debut series aims to mythologize the pineywoods he grew up in and welcome readers to a new chapter of modern Westerns, born of the tall tales that helped shape the genre. His writing is inspired by the history of the Lone Star State, the greater United States, and the larger-than-life heroes, gunslingers, and "black hats" that gave us the myth of the west we know and love today.

Nicholas is an owner at his family's limousin cattle ranch and first-time father with his wife of over ten years. As one of multiple generations of his family working on the Red Rock Limousin Ranch, Nicholas has put his experience into words as an author with a passion to keep timeless Western culture alive and thriving for today's readers.

www.ingramcontent.com/pod-product-compliance
Lightning Source LLC
LaVergne TN
LVHW041250110826
845146LV00005BA/1327

9798895674253